SEVEN DEADLY TEQUILAS

An Althea Rose Novel

TRICIA O'MALLEY

Lovewrite Publishing

Seven Deadly Tequilas

Editor:
Sara Lunsford,
MacKenzie Walton

If you would like to do any of the above, please seek permission first by
contacting the author at:
info@triciaomalley.com

"And remember, it's also very funny. Side by side with grief lies joy." – Fran Drescher

Chapter One

I CLAPPED MY HANDS, making the blonde-haired Real Housewife of Tequila Key jump in her seat and blink at me balefully from beneath lashes coated heavily in mascara. Keeping Missy Sue on track was like wrangling a pile of puppies, and while I usually managed her well enough, today she was trying my patience.

"Missy Sue! What is on your mind today? You're barely paying attention," I admonished my monthly client softly and pushed the tarot deck toward her once again. "What are we focusing this reading on?"

Ever since Luna and I had been featured – not to our particular joy, mind you – in several of the gossip magazines, Missy Sue had shown up faithfully each month with ever-increasing wild questions for the tarot cards. First, she'd come to try to contact her father who had recently passed. After that, she'd come back each month to ask more questions about her father. As far as I was concerned, a client could get a reading as many times as their credit card allowed, but in all reality, it was my belief that the tarot cards didn't like to be asked the same questions over and over. When I'd gently mentioned that fact to Missy Sue, she'd started bringing different questions to the table, each one more extravagant than the next, and I suspected she enjoyed telling her "ladies who lunch" crowd about her monthly meetings with her celebrity psychic.

Not that it mattered much to me – any advertising was good advertising. I could say that with a straight face now that my bikini-clad butt wasn't plastered across the gossip magazines, and my authenticity was no longer being called into question. Well, no more than usual, that is. There's something about psychics that just brings out the worst skeptics in people. I was used to my skills being put under a magnifying glass – just not typically on a national scale.

"Um, do you think Sheena is going to divorce Bryson?" Missy Sue picked up the cards, and I rolled my eyes, stopping her.

"We've talked about this, Missy Sue."

"Oh, right. I have to ask questions about my own life."

"Yes, you're meant to do a reading for you. You can't use tarot to get the gossip on other people in town."

"Fine." Missy Sue sighed, winding a strand of blonde hair around her finger, nails tipped in coral pink, and then brightened. "Okay, got it. Will my father's grave get robbed?"

Well, *that* was certainly a new one. Blowing out a breath, I counted to three and then looked over at my skeleton, Herman, who sported a Pink Floyd T-shirt today, and wondered if I should just cancel Missy Sue's appointment. She was clearly not focused, and my patience was wearing thin. Not like I'd ever been thick on patience, and wasn't that a weird thought? Trying to visualize what the thickness and thinness of patience would look like, I pulled myself back and refocused on Missy Sue, who was looking at me expectantly. *Now* who was the one not focused?

"Missy Sue…what on earth are you talking about?"

"You know, because of the grave robber in town?" Missy Sue leaned over, her pretty face lighting up as much as it could under the layers of Botox, and she lowered her voice to a hush. "You haven't heard?"

"No, I haven't heard."

"I'm shocked. I thought scary stuff like that would come right to you. Since you're into death and all that…" Missy Sue gave Herman a look.

"I'm not into death, Missy Sue. I simply understand there are spirits among us and know that our reality is not all that we see."

"Is there one here now?" Missy Sue looked around wildly.

"One what?" I asked, my mind on the grave robber.

"A spirit?

"Oh." I looked up and saw Rosita, a ghostly madam, waft through the divider that separated my area from Luna's shop. "Yup, sure is."

"There is? Where?" Missy Sue's eyes widened to the size of saucers, and a light sheen of sweat broke out on her upper lip.

"Missy Sue. It's fine. Spirits exist around us. They don't want to hurt us. Now, your time is running short… anything else you'd like to ask?" I nudged the cards again. Missy Sue shot to her feet when a book from my shelf tumbled off, and it took everything in my power not to yell at a grinning Rosita.

"Was that a ghost?"

"Nope, just cheap shelves," I lied, and shot a quick glare at Rosita, who made a very unladylike gesture back in my direction.

"Uh, well, so...I started selling a new line of all-natural cleaning products. Do you see me being success-ful?" Missy Sue finally focused, shuffling the cards duti-fully, while darting quick glances over her shoulder at the book that had landed on the ground next to her.

"That's a great question to ask," I said, watching as she cut the cards into three piles. Reaching for the cards, I quickly dealt out a simple Celtic Cross spread and exam-ined the cards while Missy Sue looked on hopefully. The cards, surprisingly, indicated she would be. With an eye on the clock, I ran through the reading quickly and was happy to see the flush of pleasure that crossed Missy Sue's face.

As she packed her bag to leave, I stopped her. "What about this grave robber now?"

"Oh, well, I can't believe you haven't heard! It's all everyone is talking about."

Her everyone and *my* everyone varied greatly, so I wasn't entirely shocked I hadn't heard the news yet. "I've been busy."

"Well, two graves have been robbed at the cemetery out by the highway now. Right by that godawful sign?"

Years ago, an intrepid mayor had thought to put a sign proclaiming, "Tequila Makes It Better," hoping to draw tourists to our little downtown. Instead, tourists paused for a photo and continued on their way to the party town of Key West.

"Yup, I know the cemetery. So, the graves are being robbed for...jewelry?"

"No! That's the shocking thing." Missy Sue held a hand to her heart and dropped her voice again. "The bodies have gone missing."

"No way." Even that was shocking for me, and I'd seen some wildly unusual things in the last year, the likes of which would blow one blonde Missy Sue's mind.

"Way. They're keeping it hush-hush. I only know because Melodie is friends with Angela, who was on a date with Chief Thomas when he got the call."

I didn't want to think about the Chief dating. No, I really didn't. I'd much rather think about dead bodies being stolen, so I wasn't sure what that said about me as a person.

"Two bodies have been stolen from the grave, and we know nothing else yet?"

"I'll text you any updates I get if you'd like?" Missy Sue shot a glance to Herman again. "Or maybe not..."

"It's not me, Missy Sue. I have no interest in or use for actual dead bodies. You know Herman isn't real. The concept of someone stealing them freaks me out as much as it does you."

"That's what I thought." Missy Sue bobbed her head repeatedly, and I could tell that was definitely not what she'd been thinking. "See you next month?"

"Yup, I look forward to it," I said, watching her push through the screen to Luna's shop to moon over some of her new bath products. Standing, I stared at the wall for a moment as my brain scrambled to make sense of what I'd just learned.

"Vacuous twit," Rosita said from the corner, and I shot a glance over my shoulder at her.

"Irrespective of such, we've talked about you harassing my clientele. I do need to make a living, as you well know. Or I can't keep Hank in dog bones." Rosita loved Hank, my Boston Terrier, mainly because he harassed the living hell out of the other ghost that terrorized our lives, Rafe.

"Fine, I'll be better. I promise. Are you going to look into this grave robber?"

"Nope, I most certainly am not." I put extra emphasis on the word *not* as I pulled out a fresh pack of tarot cards and put the deck Missy Sue had used to the side to clear its energy later.

"Uh-huh."

"I swear I'm not. I want nothing to do with it. I want to live a calm and normal life."

"Normal, right," Rosita said, and blinked away as my next client knocked at the door.

My name's Althea Rose, and I co-own the Luna Rose Potions & Tarot Shop in sleepy Tequila Key, and I suspected I'd just walked into another problem that our chief of police was going to need my help to solve.

So much for calm…

Chapter Two

AFTER A PARTICULARLY DIFFICULT reading wherein I had to remind the client several times that I couldn't just keep drawing more tarot cards until she received the answer that she was looking for – and if I'm totally honest, I didn't even need to use my psychic abilities to interpret her question, as half the town had seen her boyfriend making out with the new waitress at the café – I was ready to close. It wasn't my job to gossip, nor was it in me to violate my ethics to do a fake reading, so all I could do was look on helplessly while my client became increasingly agitated.

"Rough one?" Luna asked when I pushed my way through the screen into her side of the shop. My shop was more like a rock concert, whereas stepping into hers was like attending the symphony. Soothing layers of white and gold were mirrored around the room, and the natural elements of crystals, driftwood, and polished shells picked up on the earthly parts of her craft. Luna, looking as ethereal and delicate as always, shimmered in a white shift dress shot through with strands of silver. At the end of the day, not a smudge of dust on her dress or a piece of hair dared to be out of place. I knew she used magick to keep her appearance together, and it still rankled that she refused to admit it or teach me the spell so I could use it on myself.

Glancing down at my lavender maxi dress, I sighed to see a long streak of dirt across my stomach. Likely from when I leaned over my bookshelves to restack my tarot decks and bring the fresh ones forward – no matter how often I dusted, and it wasn't all that often – dust was a constant problem in Tequila Key. I swiped a hand across a table with a hand-woven basket that carried a collection of tumbled agates and sniffed when it came back clean. I really needed to learn Luna's cleaning spells.

"Yes, my client refused to believe the reading and insisted I keep drawing cards. When I refused, because you know the cards don't like that, she started crying."

"I don't know why Jade is so shocked by this. Most of the town has seen her man out with that new waitress."

"Don't I know it. Nevertheless, she's now mad at me and promised me she would never come again."

Luna scrunched up her pretty face as she thought about that. "I can't decide if that's a bad thing."

"Honestly?" I shrugged. "Me either. I'm so booked up that I can't be bothered one way or the other over clients who just want to call me a fake or whatever because they can't see what's in front of their face."

"Her pain is real, though." Luna, ever the soft-hearted one, met my eyes.

"I know, I know, I know." I pinched the bridge of my

nose with my fingers and sighed. "I gave her some rituals to do at home. Mainly things that are actually just self-empowerment and meditation type acts, but hopefully it will raise her spirits and give her enough backbone to deal with what's in front of her face."

"That's good of you. Next time send her through for one of my new baskets." Luna nodded to her front table, and I wandered over to look.

Luna, a white witch, infused all of her herbal remedies and crystals with an extra layer of magick, and she did a bustling online business as well. I picked up one basket, labeled "Inner Strength," and poked around in it. With a variety of crystals, a mandala necklace, and affirmation cards – it was a lovely collection of positive gifts.

A laugh escaped when I pulled out the last item in the bottom of the basket – a small bottle of tequila.

"Tequila?"

"Courage comes in all forms. Sometimes we need the liquid form." Luna laughed at me from across the store.

It was part of why I loved her – she could temper her new-age mysticism and magick with a dose of hard realism. I was forever grateful she'd chosen me as her best friend.

"That's my favorite kind."

"Shall we indulge in some ourselves? We may need it if the rumors are true." Luna stacked her receipts neatly and zipped a money bag shut before disappearing into her backroom to store the contents in her safe protected both by magick and a security system. While her front room only had a touch of the mystical, if a person was ever allowed in the back, they'd see the true workings of a magickal genius. From the rug that pulled back to reveal the seven-sided faery star to the carefully curated and categorized ingredients shelves, Luna was at the top of her game. She'd dragged me along with her – reluctantly, I might add – and I was slowly learning that I had certain talents that extended beyond my psychic abilities.

Well, talent may be too strong of a word for it. Unbridled abilities? A toddler with two cups of coffee in him? Either way, let's just say I still had a lot to learn.

"About the grave robber?"

"Indeed," Luna said, coming back out of the backroom and flipping the light switches off. I waited as she moved about the room, checking her physical and magickal locks before stopping at the front door. At the end of the day, I always exited with her, having already deadbolted my shop from inside. And, I'll admit, after the last few months we had, it just felt safer to leave the shop together.

Stepping out on the little porch, I glanced around just to make sure there was nothing weird about – we'd had everything from paparazzi to activists pass through lately. "All clear," I said to Luna.

"You can't possibly think the paparazzi are still following us, Althea." Luna leveled a look at me before sliding her Chanel sunglasses on.

"I'm not looking for paparazzi."

"Liar. Althea Rose, has fame gone to your head? Do you miss seeing your face in those ratty magazines of yours?"

"It's hard to miss seeing your face if they only posted pictures of your butt," I grumbled. I'd admit, that one still stung. Every other one of my friends had been featured with flawless photos, and they'd caught me in my old barely-there bikini that I'd wear under my wetsuit to go scuba diving. Let's just say the rest should be left to imagination. It was not what one would call a flattering angle.

"You have a very nice butt, Althea."

"Well, there's certainly a lot of it to look at. And even better in high-resolution photographs. Which every woman loves… "

"I'd thought you moved past this. What's up with you?" Luna stopped by her car while I unlocked my beach cruiser bicycle.

"Something's in the air. Makes me feel like I can't get back to a normal routine."

"Have you considered that maybe this is our new normal?" Luna slid in her car and gave me a jaunty *beep-beep* with her horn before zipping away. She did love to leave me with deep thoughts and a dramatic exit. It would be annoying if I didn't love her so much. Frankly, she was likely right.

I mulled it over as I biked home in the sluggish heat, like a warm, wet blanket wrapped around me, and waved to the few neighbors who sat in the shade of their porches hoping to catch a breeze. The weather had recently slipped past hot to oppressive, and the already slow pace of Tequila Key all but crawled to a halt during this time of year. I biked as slowly as I could without toppling over, my mind on Luna's words.

Things had changed since the magazine article had come out, and the subsequent drama surrounding the reality show and the crazy producer. People looked at Luna and me differently, and we'd become local celebrities in our own right. Miss Elva had catapulted her fifteen minutes of fame into a burgeoning fashion line, and even I was impressed with her designs. I'd always had a deep appreciation for Miss Elva's fashion sense, but had never felt like I could pull off what she wore. Now, after looking over some of her designs, I could see where she'd diluted some of her intensity down to a more wearable version for a client like me. She'd thought of everything.

So, if this was our new normal, did that mean I should just jump right into figuring out about a grave robber? A shudder rippled through me as I thought about the grossness that came with anything to do with that act. What was wrong with people? What desperation could drive people to disturb the dead just to steal?

I pedaled down my lane, my house tucked at the end of a long row of semi-detached houses. I loved where I lived, and had invested significant time and money in creating a space that was uniquely my own. One which I was coming to learn that I had trouble sharing with others. More specifically – a boyfriend.

I sighed as I pulled to a stop in front of my house, my brakes squeaking and reminding me I needed to oil them. Two pointy ears popped up at the window, and Hank's bark welcomed me home. It was my favorite part of the day – well, on days I didn't take him to the shop with me – and I loved nothing more than coming home and spending some time recharging after talking all day. And what better way to recharge than with the cuddliest and cutest dog in the world? Granted, all dogs were the cuddliest and cutest dogs in the world, but maybe mine was just a smidge cuter – in my completely unbiased opinion, of course.

Hank ran in ecstatic loops around my legs and then, unable to control himself, he raced to the back door, skidding across the wood floors, and then raced back to me before sliding and barreling into my legs. Laughing, I bent over and scooped him up, letting him lick my face madly, and walked over to his toy drawer.

"Okay, buddy, what toy should we pick today?"

Hank leaned forward over my arms and snuffled his nose around in the drawer before pulling out a stuffed zombie toy.

"A zombie? Really? I hope that isn't a warning sign or anything," I laughed, and tugged it from his mouth before putting him gently on the floor. Launching the zombie across the room, I smiled as Hank scrambled for it and poured myself a glass of sweet tea before making my way to the covered back patio for our after-work routine.

Sighing, I lowered myself onto my outdoor couch, situated nicely to catch the breeze from the large bamboo leaf fans, and waited for Hank to tear outside with the zombie in his mouth. Racing to me, he dropped it at my feet and barked once, demanding I throw it. I complied, knowing I would be doing so for the next hour, and was content to just relax, not look at my phone, and watch my dog race across the back yard in his after-work "zoomies" session.

I loved my life, even if it was a weird one, and it still bothered me that I struggled with sharing my space with someone else. Trace, my most recent boyfriend and best friend, had gotten as close as anyone to becoming a permanent fixture in my home and in my bed. And, *yet.* I knew it was my fault for keeping him at arm's length. At the same time, I still had some unresolved feelings for Cash, another recent boyfriend of mine.

Because I didn't feel all that great about hopping between the two of them – not like cheating, mind you, but just not committing seriously to either – I'd finally come to a decision.

I was going to date me for a while.

I laughed out loud at that and tossed the zombie again for a delirious Hank, who zipped after it with a series of delighted snorts. Okay, so saying I was going to date me sounded ridiculously new age or like when Gwyneth Paltrow decided to "consciously uncouple."

It was more like I was putting myself in a time out until I figured out how to behave like an adult.

And who knew how long that would really take?

Chapter Three

I CHANGED MY CLOTHES, ditching one maxi dress for another – this one in deep emerald green and made of the lightest, most breathable cotton – and piled my hair on my head in a loose bun. Its current color had almost faded out, so my hair looked more rose gold than anything. Adding some shimmery hammered gold earrings to my look, I quickly glanced in the mirror.

Maybe it was time for a new tattoo, I thought, as I studied the Celtic tattoo on the inside of my arm where an evil eye was incorporated in the design to ward off bad energy. Sometimes I had to wonder if it actually attracted bad energy – I needed to consult with Luna about what symbol I could get for my other arm, as it was clear I needed a double dose of protection. Especially if we continued on this path of "new normal" we were apparently on.

Hank seemed extra energetic tonight, even with the heat, so I decided to take him with me to Lucky's. Beau didn't mind when I brought him in as it was an open-air bar and restaurant, and Hank was better behaved than many of the patrons who wandered their way into the bar.

Taking in mind the heat, we wandered slowly to the bar, and Hank enjoyed his time having what I liked to call a "sniffari." Which largely consisted of him sniffing everything that he came across, thus doubling the time it would normally take to get to Lucky's. I didn't mind, though, as it was Hank's walk too, and frankly just too damn hot to muster anything faster than a slow amble across the pavement.

Was it a waddle? Was I waddling now? I pinched my stomach to see if I'd added any extra layers of late, but all seemed to be as soft and round as usual.

When we finally reached Lucky's, Hank stopping to christen the potted palm by the door, and after glancing inside to see if Beau had caught us, I made my way to where Luna was perched at the bar.

"Hank!" Luna exclaimed, sliding from her seat and dropping to her knees so an ecstatic Hank could express his undying devotion to Luna. I narrowed my eyes at her pale lavender slip dress and my black dog, and watched for any stray hairs landing on her dress. When none did, I shook my head. I knew my dog. I knew his fur. And I knew that there wasn't a light fabric in the world that would walk away unscathed. She *totally* used magick.

"Hey buddy." Beau leaned over the bar and Hank dutifully sat, raising one paw, as Beau held a treat down to him. He kept a stash of treats for his dog patrons behind the bar, which in turn earned him the gratitude of patron and dogs alike. There weren't many people who didn't like Beau, I thought, as I studied him – between his easy-going affability, handsome looks, and highly intelligent mind, there wasn't much *to* dislike about him. Well, unless you were someone who struggled to understand that gay people deserved equal rights. In that case, you'd probably find fault with everything Beau was and miss out on his sheer awesomeness.

"He seemed extra bouncy tonight, so I brought him in for some stimulation."

"Well, he's sure to get a lot of attention as there's fresh gossip for people to come in and cackle about," Beau said, nodding to the locals streaming through the door. It was inevitable in a small town. When there was gossip to be had, head to the local pub for details. It just turned out that our local pub was a tiki hut on a rocky beach. To each their own...

Hank went on alert at my feet and ran around me so fast that he wrapped the leash twice around my legs before lunging. I grabbed the bar, gasping as he almost toppled me to the floor.

"Hank! Stay!" I ordered, looking down at my feet and trying to untangle myself from the leash, when a hand, warm at my back, paused me.

"Just hold on, Althea. I got it," Trace said, his voice at my ear, and I felt a delicious shiver work its way through me. Okay, so it wasn't lack of chemistry that had been the issue with Trace and me. If the heat spreading through my nether regions was any indication, that is.

I waited, my face heating, as Trace rescued me from my predicament and crouched at my feet so Hank could shower him with the very best Hank kisses he could give. Suddenly finding myself jealous of my dog, I turned my head away and reminded myself that I was a strong independent woman who didn't need a man.

"Althea," Trace said, standing and meeting my eyes. It was the first time we'd seen each other since we'd broken things off while I was in the Bahamas, and he was off on a yacht with a bunch of lithe beauties. I hadn't prepared myself for our first run-in, and now here we were.

"Trace," I said back, nodding briskly at him. Should I hug him? I really wanted to hug him. He was my best friend before anything else.

"Oh, for Pete's sake, you two have done the dirty. Just hug and stop acting like strangers," Beau said from behind me.

I looked to the ceiling, debating whether killing myself or killing Beau made more sense right now. Trace, being Trace, laughed and leaned in for a hug.

"I've missed you, Althea," he said.

I buried my face in my spot by his neck, just for a moment, and breathed in the scent of Trace. He always smelled like the sea, which I loved, and I realized how much I missed diving in the mornings with him.

"I've missed you, too." I pulled back and gave him a genuine smile, "This is weird and awkward, and I get that. But I still love you and miss you."

"I'm used to awkward with you," Trace said, sliding into the seat next to mine.

I let out a little sigh of relief. There, everything was somewhat back to normal.

"How was your trip, Trace?" Luna asked, leaning across me to pat Trace's arm.

"It was good. Nice to dive on some different reefs."

I bristled at the thought – was that euphemism for sleeping with other women? Then I reminded myself, that I had been exploring my own reefs with Cash, and thought it best not to throw stones in this glass house of mine.

"I bet. See anything cool?" I asked.

"A whale shark. And some manta rays that I loved."

"Ohhhh, that's awesome," I breathed, and we spent the next ten minutes talking about all the various sea creatures that Trace had seen on his trip. By the time we'd finished, we were halfway through our first round of drinks, everyone was back to acting normal, and I thought I'd successfully navigated the first post break-up meeting well. Just so long as I didn't lose my head and ask him to come home with me tonight, I scolded myself.

"What's that look?" Beau asked, leaning in front of me as I eyed my dark and stormy cocktail.

"Not too strong with these, mmkay?" I tapped my glass.

"Roger that," Beau said, his eyes dancing. He knew exactly what I was on about.

"Why do you still let Theodore in here?" I complained, changing the subject and nodding to where the resident blowhard, Theodore Whittier, held court at a table across the room. No matter how many times that man was embarrassed or proven wrong, he sprang up, like a weed, and continued to infest our town with his un-asked-for opinions.

"What grounds do I have to kick him out?" Beau crossed his arms over his chest and looked around, his eyes always scanning the bar for the next drinks to be made.

"He's a liar?" Luna asked.

"He's an arrogant prick?" I suggested.

"He's small-minded?" Trace asked.

Beau shook his head and stood straight, having spied customers who needed his attention. "If I kicked everyone out for any of those traits, I could lose half my clientele. He'll need to do a lot more than that before I ban him from here."

"Hmmm…" I began to plot in my head, and Beau shot me a look over his shoulder as he crossed the bar.

"Don't even think about it, Althea. Tonight's already going to be busy. I don't want any drama."

"No drama. Got it," I made my eyes really big and nodded slowly at him, and he sighed and bent to grab two glasses tucked behind the bar.

"Don't go picking fights, Althea. I thought you wanted a normal life?" Luna poked me in the leg.

"Oh. Right. Normal."

"Like that's gonna happen." Trace snorted next to me and took a slug of his beer.

"Well, hey, maybe my normal is different than other people's normal." I shrugged.

"Oh, it is. Trust me. It is." Trace laughed, but patted my arm to let me know he wasn't being mean. That was typical of Trace. He'd poke fun, but always check to make sure he hadn't crossed the line into being mean.

"Speaking of not normal…" Luna leaned in. "It appears we have a new criminal in Tequila Key."

"Oh no. What now? I've been on the boat all day," Trace said, nodding to Beau, who had motioned to his now empty beer.

"The word on the street is that we have a grave robber," I said, and filled him in on the few details that Missy Sue had been able to supply.

"Gross," Trace said succinctly, nodding his thanks to Beau, who dropped an ice-cold bottle of beer in front of him and whisked the empty away. I was grateful for the large fans Beau had installed under the thatched roof of the tiki hut, or I'd be sweltering. An ice-cold beer was even beginning to look tasty to me, and I was not a beer person.

"It is gross. And unethical. And breaks a lot of moral and magickal rules," Luna said. Trace knew what we were, so we never had to hide our discussions of magick from him. "Last rites matter. Being laid to rest matters. Whether it's a religious last rite, a magickal one, or non-denominational, there's something specific and binding to laying a body to rest. It's not right to disturb that."

"No, it's really not. And, as Trace said so eloquently – it's gross."

"Yeah, that too." Luna scrunched her pretty nose up delicately. She looked like a little doll when she made that expression, and I looked like I'd eaten a bad egg.

"What does Miss Elva say about it?" Trace asked.

"She's getting back today, I believe," I said, looking to Luna, who confirmed with a nod.

"How's she doing with that new man of hers?"

"Good, I think. She was sending me photos every day of her lounging in her sparkle bikini on a flamingo float in the pool."

"Ah…hmmm." Trace shook his head at the image.

"Did I mention quite often topless?" I asked, really wanting to paint the picture for him.

"Oh man," Trace laughed, "I love that woman."

"Goddess above, but so do I. If I could bottle an ounce of her confidence and drink it every day, I'd take over the world." Just thinking about Miss Elva made me smile.

"You have no reason not to be as confident as her, Althea. You're stunning," Trace said, a bit of sadness reaching the corner of his eyes as he studied me.

"Thank you," I said, keeping my tone light, and reaching out, I squeezed his hand. "I'm working on it. Which is why I've decided to date myself for a while."

"Oh, well, bless your heart," Luna said from my other side, and I believed she was speaking in Southern to tell me she thought I was crazy.

"What's she doing now?" Beau asked, having caught Luna's comment as he delivered fresh drinks and another treat for Hank.

"She's dating herself," Luna supplied happily, and I groaned.

"Is that a fancy way of saying you're single?"

"I believe so," Trace laughed.

"Can't you just say you're single? Why do you have to put a label on it like it's a meditation retreat you're trying out? We all do this, Althea. We are in relationships or out of relationships. That's life." Beau rolled his eyes.

"I just meant I'm choosing to stay alone until I can figure my shit out." I sighed and buried my face in my drink.

"Well, you certainly won't find answers there, if being in the bar business has taught me anything." Beau nodded to my drink.

"So, Beau, did you hear about the grave robber?" I

asked brightly, widening my eyes at him in a very clear *Let's change the subject or I'll strangle you* look.

"I did, yes. It seems they found another grave open today."

"How many is that now?"

"That's five graves robbed," Beau said.

"How come they don't just put a guard on the cemetery at night until this is over?" Luna asked.

"I believe they have. But they are distracted somehow every evening. Last night it was from a small explosion outside the cemetery. The guard goes looking, and the thief sneaks in the other way."

"Are you sure they aren't stealing the bodies for jewelry? Or maybe for the organs? I really don't understand," I mused, sipping my cocktail and enjoying the bite of ginger in my drink.

"For some jewelry? No, no." Beau looked at all of us in disbelief. "I'm sure you've heard by now."

"Missy Sue mentioned it wasn't for jewelry, but I always need to vet her rumors." I said.

"Hear what?" Luna asked.

"The grave robber isn't stealing jewelry. He's stealing the bodies."

"Extra-gross." Trace shook his head in disgust.

I had to agree.

Chapter Four

HANK and I wandered our way home after we finished our last round of drinks and I had finished devouring chicken fingers from the kid's menu, much to Beau's chagrin. I applauded myself for not ordering French fries with it, thinking that counted as a protein-rich healthy dinner. Luna politely didn't say anything as she ate her Caesar salad, Trace only smiled at me, and we all left with parting hugs. All things considered, I thought the night had been a success, even if I did linger in Trace's arms for a moment longer than necessary when he hugged me.

Enjoying the light breeze and the slightly cooler temperature, I turned down Miss Elva's street on a whim, letting Hank take his time as he made sure every dog on this street would know he had been there.

"For a streetwalker, you need to work on your outfits."

Turning my head, I glared at where Rafe, Miss Elva's pirate ghost, hovered at her front porch. "I'm not a street-walker, Rafe. I'm walking my dog."

"Looks suspicious to me," Rafe sniffed.

Technically, he wasn't wrong. I was out walking, and I had been on the street. But I didn't feel like giving Rafe even an inch when it came to things like this. It only encouraged him.

Hank tugged at his leash, looking back at me.

"Go say hi, Hank." I smiled sweetly and dropped the leash, and Hank lunged after Rafe, who shrieked and zipped into a corner of the porch.

"Now, who is my sweet angel baby? Who is the cutest doggo to ever dog?" Miss Elva bent from where she sat on her rocker in the dark corner of the porch and pet an adoring Hank. Rafe hissed at him from behind her shoulder and Rosita zipped up to laugh at him.

"I can't believe he's still scared of that dog. Hank is the sweetest," Rosita said, perching on the porch and crossing her legs.

"Rafe doesn't exactly have balls of steel, as we would say," I said, climbing the steps and leaning against the porch railing.

"Or much of anything down there, really, at least according to the girls at my brothel." Rosita studied one of her nails.

"Heathen! How dare you!" Rafe screeched, and even Miss Elva turned on him.

"Rafe, you're going to have to bring your volume level down. As in now. I don't need you screaming in my ear like a banshee. Pull yourself together."

"Yes…my…lovemountain," Rafe said, and I was shocked to see his shoulders shake before he zipped around the backyard.

"Was he crying?" I asked incredulously. Rafe was

prone to dramatics, but they usually leaned heavily on the anger side.

"Rafe's still a little sensitive about my new man." Miss Elva shrugged.

I took the time to study her. Her silver caftan glimmered in the moonlight, and a sparkle headband added an extra fun touch. She looked relaxed – softer even – and a smile hovered around her lips.

"That's because the King knows how to please a woman," Rosita said.

I shuddered slightly at the visual of the Flamingo King…well, I'd just let the rest of that thought lie.

"That he does, girl, that he does," Miss Elva chuckled.

"Rafe's not handling it well? I thought you had an agreement."

"We do. But I think he was comfortable with me just having lovers before. This time he thinks it is more and that I'll forget him."

"You will!" Rafe wailed from around the corner of the house, and Miss Elva waved her hand in the air and sighed.

"Men and their fragile egos." Rosita shook her head sadly.

"Hush, you strumpet!" Rafe shouted.

"He's definitely…louder."

Hank propped his paws on the porch railing to tilt his head around the corner at Rafe.

"Devil beast," Rafe hissed.

"Rafe, either hang out on the porch or go away," I said.

"You do not tell me what to do."

"Rafe, you're making me hurt my neck with all the

zipping about you're doing. Get on the porch or go inside. Can't you see I'm trying to have a nice conversation with Althea? I haven't seen her in weeks." Miss Elva scolded.

"Like she has anything interesting to say," Rafe sniffed, and settled himself on the porch but out of range of Hank.

"*Lovely* to have you back, Rafe." I beamed at him. "Miss Elva, how was your vacation? How is the Flamingo King doing?"

"He's had a rough go of it, child, that's the truth of it. It's hard to lose someone you thought was family, you know? But he's doing better. He's decided to throw himself into work and close up all the loose ends and shady employees that had snuck into his organizations. I helped him with who to keep and who to get rid of. He seems happier keeping busy, and is off to visit his manufacturing plants to make sure everything is in tip-top shape."

"Are you guys a couple? Or how will you handle long distance? This is new territory for you."

Miss Elva leveled me a look. "Honey, this is not new territory for me. I've been in long-term relationships before. I just haven't for a while because I enjoy eating from the buffet, if you get my drift."

"Yup, got it," I said, shaking my head to clear that particular image out. "I guess I'm just curious because I have no handle on my love life at all."

"Maybe you're not meant to handle it at all right now." Miss Elva shrugged one silvery shoulder. "But as for me and mine, we've decided to not be exclusive. But we'll visit each other when in the mood, and we still message and talk. I don't think he's ready to lose a friend or confidant, but he's also not in a place to start a relationship."

"How do you feel about that?"

"I'm fantastic. I love being with a man, but I also love my freedom. It's nice to be back in my space."

"Would you ever share your space with a partner?"

"Have you seen my house?"

"Yes, it's amazing and kind of like a magickal museum."

"It's my space. I'm not sharing."

"I wish I could be as clear on that point as you are."

"You haven't been giving yourself any time to figure it out, bouncing from man to man like you do."

"Whore," Rafe mumbled, and I shot him a glare.

"Hank, get Rafe!"

Hank jumped up and tore down the porch after Rafe, who shrieked once more and disappeared around the house.

"I have no idea why he shames women for having a healthy sexual life," Rosita mused. "He was at my brothel every night he could afford to be."

"Double standards. Also, what's wrong with bouncing from man to man? Didn't you just say you like to eat from the buffet?"

"I do. But that's me." Miss Elva pointed a finger at herself. "I'm much older than you. I'm not looking to marry or start a family."

"Eeeek," I said, shivering at the thought of having kids. If I couldn't even share my house with a boyfriend, how would I share it with a child? "Nobody said anything about having babies."

"I'm just saying that I am comfortable with my choices to sample all the dessert. I don't know if that's for you. I think eventually you're going to settle down with someone."

"Maybe. Maybe not. I'm taking some me time right now."

"That's not a bad thing to do, child. Get your head on straight. Do some affirmations. Go to a yoga retreat. Get a massage."

"Who are you, and what have you done with Miss Elva?" I asked, tilting my head at her.

"Honey, I'm just relaxed. Several weeks of good loving will do that to a woman. Now I'm back to dive into my business and I'm in a relaxed mood. All is well here."

"Except it's not."

"I knew it!" Miss Elva thumped her foot on the ground. "I could feel it in the air tonight. And the moon has a pink shadow. Who died?"

"Um, well, they were already dead, but we have a grave robber in town."

"A pirate!" Rafe zipped back around.

"No, not a pirate. A robber."

"That's what pirates do, wench," Rafe said, rolling his eyes at me.

"Well, this particular robber is not taking jewelry and gold; he's stealing the dead bodies." I put my hands on my hips. "Is that what you did, Rafe? Steal bodies?"

"Why steal bodies? You just toss them in the ocean for the fish to eat."

"That's not good. Not good at all." Miss Elva made a

tsking noise with her mouth. "I don't like hearing that bodies are missing."

"Yeah, that seems to be the general consensus. Any idea what they would be doing with them?"

"Mmm, there's many a dark magick that can be used with dead bodies. Likely a necromancer. Or zombies. But zombies usually take the living."

"Excuse me?" My breath whooshed out of me and I sagged against the railing. "You're thinking zombies? I didn't know they were actually real."

"Of course they are real, child. Where did you think Hollywood comes up with all those movies?"

"Um, from their imagination?" Goddess above, there had better not be zombies in Tequila Key. If so, I was taking Hank and we were going for an extended vacation.

"You have a lot to learn," Miss Elva said. "And I do not have the energy to teach you all of it tonight. Keep an eye out. Be safe. Listen for heavy breathing. That kind of stuff."

"Um, I am so not liking this. I still have to walk home!"

"I don't think they like dogs. You'll be fine."

"Well, on that note, I'm leaving before it gets any later and I get eaten by a zombie. A zombie! Yeesh." I shook my head and waved goodbye to a chuckling Miss Elva. Whistling for Hank, I was surprised to find Rosita trailing me home. "You're joining me?"

"Rafe's dramatics are bothersome. I'll take some peace and quiet at your place tonight."

"I don't blame you. He's pretty torn up."

"He's just needing attention. He'll settle down in a day or two once Miss Elva strokes his little ego."

"Men." I shrugged.

"At least they are easy to manipulate," Rosita agreed.

We didn't speak anymore after that, and I successfully made it home with no zombie attacks. After hurrying through my nighttime routine, I tucked into bed with Hank and allowed myself one hour of a *Real Housewives* show before I crashed.

Hours later, I jolted upright in my bed due to Hank's hysterical barking.

"Hank!" I shouted, flipping on the light and realizing he was barking from downstairs. He must have left the bed at some point, which was highly unusual for him to do. "Hank!"

Racing downstairs in just my tank top and underwear, I hit the wall switch to flood the living area with light. Hank stood at the back door, teeth bared, hackles raised, and let loose the nastiest growl I have ever heard him emit.

"Hank?" I whispered, approaching him and then stopping dead in my tracks as what he was growling at came into view.

A man stood at the back door, bumping his head – which was barely still attached – listlessly into the glass door. His arms flailed at his side, and chunks of skin were missing so you could see the bones inside of him. On his next *thunk* against the door, his face tilted up, and now it was time for me to scream when I saw his eyes were missing.

Hank let out a blistering round of barks and the… zombie creature thingie…seemed to finally focus on him.

At the sound of Hank's barks, he wheeled erratically and disappeared into the darkness of the backyard.

"Holy shit, Hank," I said, dropping to my knees and holding my arms out for my fierce little warrior dog, who came to stand in front of me, facing out, his eyes still on the back door. "I'm calling reinforcements."

Chapter Five

"SO MUCH FOR PEACE AND QUIET," Rosita said from over my shoulder, and I jumped, causing Hank to whirl and let out a stream of barks.

"I swear…you scared the shit of out of me, Rosita!"

"Oh? Not the half-decomposed body knocking at your back door? That didn't scare you?"

"Obviously, that also scared me," I said, looking around to make sure there were no more eyeless faces staring in the window at me. "Stay with Hank, please. I'm just going to run upstairs for my phone."

"I'll protect this furry love bomb with all my might," Rosita promised.

I raced upstairs and grabbed my phone from where it was charging by my bedside, and ran back downstairs to sit on the floor by Hank. Pausing, I thought about who to call first – the police? Luna?

I did what any sane woman would do.

"Honey, you better have a good reason for waking me

from my beauty sleep at two in the morning," Miss Elva, her voice grumpy through the speaker, chastised me.

"I think I have a zombie in my backyard."

"That's a good reason," Miss Elva agreed, and I could hear her moving, "I swear. I'm not even home a day. A day! This town would go to hell without me around to take care of things. I'm surprised I was even able to stay away for a few weeks. Damn town could've burned down without Miss Elva on the watch. And look, look what's happened in my absence. A grave robber has stirred up all sorts of trouble. You'd think I could come home and have a moment of peace."

"Uh-huh. So, you're coming? What should I do? Do I go outside? Do I stay away from the windows?"

"Althea Rose. Do not go outside until I get there. Like I need to rescue you, too. You'd better keep your butt in one spot until I come knocking on your door, you hear me? I don't have time or energy for you causing any more problems on top of this."

"Yes, ma'am." Since I had zero interest in going outside to play with a dead man, I was inclined to surrender to her orders and ignore the implied criticism that I couldn't handle my shit. I mean, I could handle my shit. Mostly. But my track record of late perhaps didn't inspire the most confidence in my friends.

"I mean it. Be there in ten."

And that was a good friend, I thought, nuzzling Hank while I called Luna. Miss Elva and I had gone through a few ups and downs in our friendship, but ultimately, she and I had a bond that would last through the tough spots.

"What's wrong?" Luna asked immediately, and I could

hear her boyfriend, Mathias, murmuring in the background.

"A dead body came knocking on my back door."

"Be there in fifteen."

There you had it. Friends that would come over in a heartbeat when you told them a dead man was wandering around your backyard. I honestly couldn't think who else would show up for me this way. Aside from Beau, that is, but I didn't bother to call him. He was likely still closing the bar and he had zero magickal prowess to assist in something like that.

My mind drifted to Trace, and I hovered over his name in my contact list before putting the phone back down in my lap and hugging Hank to me. If I was going to be giving myself "me" time, then I had to deal with some of these problems without immediately calling Trace.

Or Cash.

I thought about Cash and how we'd left things after the Bahamas. He'd made it clear he was interested in me again, and willing to be more open-minded about all of the magickal otherworldly stuff that I was involved in. And I genuinely liked him – goddess knew we had a sizzling chemistry – but I was still struggling with what our relationship could look like outside the bedroom. Our lives just didn't fit together, and I wasn't sure that either of us had the conviction to make it work. When we were on vacation, our time was fantastic. Yet, in some respects, we'd both known that wasn't real life. It was an escape away from everything, and once returning to normal – well, our *normal* was wildly different. We'd decided to do what we always ended up doing – splitting ways and remaining friends.

And so the world turned.

Hank's ears perked up, and he raced to the front door a full minute before a knock sounded. I jumped up and ran across the room, not wanting Miss Elva to be stuck outside with a dead man for long. "Miss Elva?"

"It's me, honey. Just let me in real quick now."

"Thank you for coming, I didn't know what to do," I said, unlocking the door and swinging it open so Miss Elva could sweep through the door. I raised my eyebrows at her dressing gown – hot pink with rose-gold ostrich feathers – and she had her hair wrapped in a soft pink turban.

"I know you don't. Which is why I'm running all over town in my dressing gown. I wouldn't do this for everyone, you know."

"I know it. You're a good friend, Miss Elva. And I'm continually impressed by your wide knowledge base. I've yet to see much that you don't know how to handle."

"Reading, love, reading." Miss Elva tapped a finger to her head. "Read more books. Less of those magazines of yours. Then, after you read the books, spend some time really thinking about them. Especially when it comes to spells and magick. There's a give and take with the magickal world. Don't just read a spell and then try to execute it. You want to think about the intent behind the spell. How does the energy flow? Is it right for what you want to accomplish? All of that stuff takes time, study, and years of practice. You'll get there if you apply yourself. Your natural power is equally as strong as mine, but your knowledge base is severely lacking."

"Thanks. I think?"

"You're welcome. I'm not one to soften the truth, especially in the middle of the night."

"Or ever, really, if we're being honest," I said, and Miss Elva hooted out a laugh before charging across the room, her gown floating behind her.

"She just called you stupid," Rafe jeered, and I turned to where he hovered by the door.

"She did not call me stupid. She said I had more to learn. There's a big difference. And, be careful, Rafe. I brought you into this world, and I can send you back over."

"Someone's cranky in the middle of the night." Rafe glowered at me. "Must not be getting loved on. Your men finally leave you?"

"I left them, Rafe. And my sex life is none of your business."

"You don't have a sex life. So there's no business to be had one way or the other."

I was saved from saying something meaner than I should have about *his* sex life by Luna knocking at the door.

"Luna, thanks for coming," I said, opening the door slightly so she could slip inside. She looked lovely, as usual, in simple cotton sleep shorts and loose button-down pajama top.

"Of course. I'm glad you called Miss Elva, she'll be needed," Luna said, giving me a quick hug before bending to pet Hank, who waited dutifully for attention.

"I can't see anything," Miss Elva said from where she stood at the back door.

"Tell me what happened," Luna asked, dropping her bag on the kitchen counter and going to stand at the door next to Miss Elva.

"I woke up to Hank barking from downstairs. I raced down here and he was at the back door having an absolute fit. I've never seen him like this before. His fur was raised. He was growling. When I threw the lights on, there was a man at the door. Like with his skin falling off and no eyeballs." I shuddered, crossing my arms over my chest. "And he kept thunking his head on the door until he seemed to register Hank's barking. When he did, he kind of flapped his arms and ran off. Well, not really ran. Lumbered? Dragged? He's not well put together."

"Good boy, Hank." Luna crouched to pet him once again. "Protecting your mama."

"I told you they don't like dogs."

"Was it actually a zombie? Because if so, I'm leaving town."

"Hard to say. The fact he left, though, indicates…" Miss Elva trailed off and looked at Luna.

"Necromancer," Luna supplied.

"Mmhmm, that was my first thought when Althea told me."

"I need a little more information," I said, and Rafe rolled his eyes at me.

"Try reading a book, Althea."

"Try getting a life, Rafe. Oh wait, you can't."

"Althea," Luna softly chided me when Rafe zipped away in a huff.

"Sorry, I'm groggy and scared." I rubbed a hand over my face. "And it's not like he's particularly nice to me."

"He'll be fine. He's used to trading barbs with her," Miss Elva promised. "Rosita? Can you do me a favor?"

"You want me to go in the backyard and see if he's still there?"

"Could you? That would be really helpful."

"I'm happy to help. Especially since the man of the house is probably crying somewhere." Rosita shook her head and drifted easily through the window, off to explore the backyard.

"The thing is...how did he get in my backyard?" I asked, crossing to stand next to the other two women. "It's completely fenced, and he didn't look to be in good enough shape to climb a fence."

"Was he wet?" Miss Elva asked.

"Ew, are you thinking a swimming zombie?" I shuddered at that particular notion.

"I don't think this is a zombie," Luna said.

"Oh, right. Necromancer. What is that again?"

"Basically, a powerful witch can pull souls and plop them into recently deceased bodies and control their movements. It's like reincarnation, but instead of the person being born again as a baby, their souls are forcibly put into recently deceased bodies. So, they aren't bringing you back as a chipmunk or something, they are just taking your soul and shoving it in the nearest available dead body."

"I find this troubling." Understatement of the year. I took a deep breath and slid a glance to my liquor cabinet. What were the rules on drinking in the middle of the night when a dead body shows up knocking? I felt like there had to be some leniency in these situations.

"No alcohol, Althea. We may need you for a spell." Miss Elva clucked her tongue.

"Oh, sure. That makes sense." I nodded, eyes widened, as though I hadn't even been thinking of reaching for the tequila.

"Did they say how many graves had been robbed already?" Miss Elva asked.

"I think a few now. They've put extra watches on at night, but the security guards always get pulled away by some well-placed distractions," Luna said.

"Have any of the bodies been found?" Miss Elva asked.

"Not that I've heard of. Luna?"

"I asked Mathias, and nothing's turned up at the morgue," Luna said. "So far, the bodies still are missing."

"What's the point? I mean…like why would someone do this? Just because they can? It doesn't really sound all that fun to me. I mean, there's some really cool magick to be done, and picking something like raising half-decomposed bodies just is not up there on my list of cool things. Like, use magick to build you a secret island getaway or something. Way cooler, right?" At least, to me that sounded a lot better than mucking around in a grave with decomposing bodies.

"It's a power thing. Some people like to know that they can control the dead."

"But why? What are they going to do? Create an army or something?" I shuddered at that visual.

"It's hard to say why people with power do the things they do. But I suspect there is a deeply personal reason why this witch or wizard is doing this. It doesn't seem very organized, which speaks to me of highly charged emotions. Something's driving this."

"I wonder if we should look at …" Miss Elva began, but then Rosita popped back into the room, a grin on her face.

"Found him!"

"What's he doing?" I said, leaning forward to squint into the darkness in the backyard.

"He's dead. Drowned on your beach. Well, I guess not drowned since his lungs are gone, but you know. He's washed up on the sand, face down."

"Not moving anymore?" Luna asked.

"Nope."

"Is the soul still around?"

"He was. Briefly. A chatty fella named Nathaniel. Would have enjoyed passing some time with him, if you get my drift, but he got sucked back into the veil. I almost got pulled in with him! Just dodged that at the last second."

"Anything else in the backyard? Or any person?" Luna asked.

"Nope, all clear."

"I think you need to call the police, Althea," Miss Elva decided.

"What? No way. I'm not getting them involved. Can't I just push him into the sea?"

"Yes! Althea's finally becoming the pirate wench I knew she'd be," Rafe crowed from behind me, and I realized how morally repugnant my words had been.

"Nope, you're right. Police it is."

Chapter Six

"SHOULD WE GO TAKE A LOOK?" Luna asked.

"Do we really have to? He's not looking great; I can attest to that fact. And I suspect the smell is even worse."

Luna wrinkled her nose at the thought.

"Of course we are going to go see him. I need to see if I can read the signature on him." Miss Elva moved to unlock my sliding glass door.

"The signature?" I asked.

"Our magick carries our own imprint with it. If you're well-practiced, like Miss Elva is," Luna smiled at me and ran a hand down my arm, "and as we hope you'll get to be, you should be able to make out some discerning features of the spell. That way we can start tracing it, or if it happens again, we can see if there is more than one person working on the magick."

"Huh, I did not know this."

"It's not the easiest to do. And each person has their own way of reading a signature. For me, I can sort of see the color and aura of it. For Miss Elva…"

"It's the smell," Miss Elva said, turning to look at me. "Each spell has a signature scent. Like when someone comes into the elevator wearing too much perfume."

"I hate that."

"Me too. Don't they know people have allergies?" Miss Elva glanced down at Hank who had come to stand by the door, waiting to join us. "You want Hank inside or out with us?"

"Um, I don't know. Do you think he could get hurt by this?"

"No. Most likely, he'd scare something off. But that also might be good reason to keep him inside in case we have a perpetrator to fight."

Oh, lovely, I thought. Now we were fighting? Miss Elva in a flimsy dressing gown, Luna in her sleep shorts, and me in… I looked down at myself. Well, shit, I was still in my tank top and underwear. I hadn't even thought to put on clothes yet. Neither of my friends had mentioned it.

"Let's keep him inside. Sorry, I don't really have clothes on."

"More clothes than that raggedy old bikini of yours," Miss Elva sniffed.

"Oh, come on! That's my dive bikini. It goes under my wetsuit. It was never, never meant to be seen off of a dive boat. Stupid photographers and their stupid long-lens cameras," I protested.

"A woman should dress for all occasions." Miss Elva, suddenly acting like Coco Chanel in here, stuck her nose in the air. Though it was hard to argue with someone who was wearing silk and ostrich feathers to a corpse-fight in the dead of the night.

"Ladies? Shall we?" Luna stifled a yawn.

"Let the record note that I am against this decision," I said.

"It is noted. Now get your butt outside so we figure out what magick we're dealing with. Oh, and we are going to need coffee," Luna decided.

"I'll stay and make the coffee. It's the very least I can do for you coming over in the middle of the night," I offered. *Please take me up on it, please take me up on it.*

"Outside. Now," Miss Elva said.

I sighed.

"Hank, stay," I ordered, and my darling dog did exactly what I wanted to do, and went and curled up on the couch.

Following Miss Elva outside, I bent and plugged in the strand of string lights I had hung in little arcs across the fence that ran the length of my backyard, and down to my most favorite spot of the house – my secret beach. It was rare to have any waterfront space in Tequila Key – well, at least that someone like myself could afford – and I'd put time and energy into creating a small sand beach for Hank to romp in the waves.

It was there we headed now, our heads swiveling as we looked for anything else out of place in the narrow back-yard. Longer than it was wide, it was a great spot for Hank to race down to the water and back, but it certainly wasn't what one would call sprawling. If anyone was hiding back here, we'd see them easily.

"May I be the first to say that some may not consider this normal?" I said, my eyes darting everywhere as I waited for an army of zombies to climb my fence or surge out of the ocean. It didn't matter that Miss Elva was telling me we weren't dealing with zombies. I felt the nuances between the particular types of walking dead people didn't really matter at this point.

"Normal is relative. Our normal is just a bit zestier than others," Miss Elva said.

"Maybe I like less zest."

"It's good for you, Althea. Grows you as a person."

"Maybe I was fine just where I was."

"You weren't fine because you weren't using even one-tenth of your potential. Is that the life you want to live? Truly? Because you've only got one of them."

"Hey!" Rafe said from over her shoulder. "You get some extra time on the other side."

"Sorry, honey. You only get one life at a time. And that's it? You want to max out at your age – settle in and read cards and go scuba diving? You'll do that for the next fifty years?" Miss Elva looked positively fearful as she rounded on me, her eyes glittering in the light, her ostrich feathers trembling around her face.

"I understand what you are trying to tell me." I held up my hand. "I'm not saying I don't want to learn new things or try new experiences. I just hadn't thought this would be the type of experiences I'd be having." I nodded toward a lump on the beach, waves lapping gently around it.

"And? You don't always get to choose your experiences in life, child. Sometimes shit just happens to you. And you can complain about it, or you can put your big girl panties on – and remind me to discuss your underwear choices another time – and get to work. You think I'd choose to be in your garden right now, hovering over a dead body in the middle of the night when I'm jet-lagged?

No. I would *not* choose this. But my particular skill set is required, and here I am. You don't hear me complaining about it, do you?"

"No, ma'am," I said, biting my tongue to keep from pointing out that she sounded dangerously close to complaining. Not to mention the fact that the Bahamas was about an hour flight from Tequila Key, so how she thought she was jet-lagged was beyond me. I may not be the brightest, but I did know not to argue with a woman in her dressing gown standing over a dead body in the middle of the night.

"Great. Now hush up so I can do some diagnosing." Miss Elva waved me away, and I hung back as she and Luna stepped close to where the body lay on the sand.

"She told *you*," Rafe whispered over my shoulder. Even he knew when not to mess with Miss Elva and kept his voice quiet.

"Rafe…I swear…just shut it. I'm trying to learn. You just lectured me about learning, didn't you? How can I do that if you're yammering in my ear? Go be useful and scout the perimeter or something."

"Ah, the wench wants a worthy pirate to secure the perimeter. I shall do so." Rafe did love a task that boosted his ego, and I was happy to get him off my shoulder.

Narrowing my eyes a bit, I tried to see if I could determine any sort of magickal signature around the dead man. Moving closer, but not so close as to be downwind from the body, I took a few deep breaths and tried to focus.

"It smells like vanilla and lavender," Miss Elva finally said, standing over the body, which thankfully lay face down, as she sniffed.

I highly doubted that would be the smell I got if I moved any closer.

"I'm getting a purplish-gray vibe," Luna mused.

"It feels…annoying. Like the annoying kid who never stops talking and wants to play with the big boys. Or something like that."

Both women turned and looked at me, and I realized I'd spoken out loud.

"Interesting. You feel it then?" Luna beamed at me like a proud mama.

"I…um, sure? Honestly hadn't realized I'd spoken out loud." I huffed out a laugh and tugged on a wayward curl that had fallen from my topknot.

"Let it flow. See if you can examine it further," Miss Elva encouraged. "Close your eyes and let yourself feel."

"You're not going to push me in the water or something when I have my eyes closed, are you? Because I would so not be down with that." I glared at her.

"I wasn't planning on it, but now I might." Miss Elva glared right back.

"Lovely." But I shut my eyes and did as I was told. Taking a few deep breaths, which I instantly regretted due to that whole rotting flesh smell, I tried to focus on the feeling I got from the scene around me. It came to me in little bursts, the energy seemingly frenetic, and I could sense the uncertainty and urgency around the spell.

"She's new to this. Uncertain. But very urgent. Almost manically so."

"It's a she?" Luna asked.

I opened my eyes. "I honestly have no idea why I said that."

"Trust that instinct then." Miss Elva nodded with approval. "Add in my lavender-vanilla scent and Luna's purple colors and that could very well signal female. Not necessarily, as everything is quite fluid these days, but we can go with those instincts."

"So now what? What do we do with this information?"

"We make note of it. I don't think any spell is worth doing right now. If the soul has already gone back into the veil, it will be tricky to summon him back for more information."

"Which soul?" I asked. I didn't know if she meant the actual dead person's soul – may they rest in peace – or the one that had recently inhabited the body at my feet.

"The new one. Nathaniel, I think his name was. If we can get one to stay next time, we can interrogate it for more information. Souls don't care – they love to chat. So I bet we'll get lucky next time."

"Next time?" I squeaked.

"You don't think this isn't going to happen again? You said it yourself – there's a sense of urgency here. We just have to bide our time."

"Oh, right. Great. Just great."

"It's time to call the police, Althea. You can't leave him here," Luna said, reaching out to tug my arm and lead me toward the house.

"And what happens when they think it's me who did this?"

"We'll deal with it. Like we always do."

"If I call them and they take me in, can either of you watch Hank? I don't think this is going to look all that well for me." I glanced back over my shoulder at the body on the shoreline. "You're sure we can't just nudge him out into the water?"

"I mean…it's an option," Miss Elva considered. "It's not a nice option. But it's an option."

"We don't know if there are clues on there for the police," Luna countered.

"I don't think they are getting fingerprints off him. Half of him is gone and the rest is being covered in saltwater," I pointed out.

"Nevertheless, it's probably smart to call it in. Because what if you're being set up? Maybe someone took a picture of him in your backyard and is trying to frame you. Or sent info to the police already. If we don't make the call, you could be setting yourself up for trouble."

"Oh, she's right." Miss Elva nodded to me. "Luna's got a good head on her shoulders. Plus, her morals are better than mine."

"Probably mine, too," I said, and sighing, I went inside to find my phone, where I had the police programmed in. What did that say about my life that I had the chief of police's personal number in my phone?

"Chief Thomas? Sorry to wake you. It's Althea. Yeah…we've got a problem."

Chapter Seven

I LIKED Chief Thomas about as much as I could like any police officer after the old chief of police tried to kill me. I have to say, an experience like that left a lasting impression on a person.

However, as someone of authority went, I felt like Chief Thomas had been fair with me in the past, and had chosen to keep an open mind about our extrasensory abilities. Which was more than I could say for many people in Tequila Key, so I had that working in my favor. Nevertheless, I knew this didn't look good.

"Coffee?" I asked Chief Thomas, and he nodded his thanks, standing placidly in my living space in his khaki pants looking completely out of sorts amongst my colorful and decidedly eclectic decorating style. I saw him cast a glance at where my knight's armor stood in the corner by a red velvet chair.

"Please. It's a bit earlier in the morning than I'm used to rising," Chief Thomas said, pulling a notebook from his pocket.

He'd come alone, as requested, and now waited patiently for me to tell him the story. Miss Elva had vacated the premises, but Luna sat curled on the couch, having tugged on a pair of my old sweats, and sipped a cup of mint tea.

"I understand. Thank you for coming. And for coming alone. It's…ah, well, it's a tricky situation to explain," I admitted, nerves fluttering in my stomach as I thought about what I had to tell him. I poured us both a cup of coffee and leaned against the counter with mine. I had also run upstairs and put on pants, thinking it best not to greet Chief Thomas half-naked.

"Why don't you just run it through for me?"

"It's…it's hard for even me to believe, I'll admit. I don't know what you're going to think," I said, tugging on a curl of hair.

"Althea, I've dealt with your group enough now to know that not all is as it seems in this world. I'm keeping an open mind. But I can't exactly have any judgement on something unless you tell me what that something is."

Fair point.

"Okay, so I woke out of a dead sleep to Hank barking hysterically downstairs. Which is unusual for him, as he sleeps on my bed and doesn't go downstairs at night."

"What time was this?"

"I'd say like 2 to 2:30?"

"Okay, go on."

"And, well, I came downstairs and there was a dead body banging his head against my back door." I said the last part in a rush of air and waited, watching Chief Thomas carefully.

His pen paused on his paper pad, and he looked up, his blue eyes holding mine. "A dead body? How did you know it was dead?"

"Um, largely because the eyes and half of his skin were missing."

"Could be a burn victim asking for help."

"I could see through parts of him. And there was no blood."

"Ah."

Ah? Was that all he had to say? Nervous, I rushed out the rest of the story, leaving out the bits about magick and did my best to stick to the facts. "So that's about it. He's down there now. I wasn't sure what to do. And so I called you."

"He's still on the beach?"

"That I'm aware of."

"Did you touch him?" Chief Thomas was already striding to the door.

"We thought best not to touch him. We just kind of stood over him and tried to figure out what was happening."

"Come with me, Althea," Chief Thomas ordered, and then glanced back at Luna. "You too, Luna. I want your statement as well."

"Yes, sir."

Together we walked through the backyard, not saying a word. The sun was just cresting the horizon, the breeze was light, and otherwise it would have been a beautiful morning. There was something special about the stillness of these early mornings where the air was still cool and the water looked like glass. I knew that many people in

Tequila Key got up earlier during the hot season to enjoy this time in their gardens before the heat settled in.

We all paused at where the body lay, now half-submerged in the rising tide, and studied it.

"Has he moved?"

"No, this is how we found him."

Chief Thomas sighed and squatted by the body, reaching automatically to test the pulse and then drawing his hand away when his fingers went right into the bones of the neck. "Okay, he's definitely dead and has been for a while. Did you recognize the person?"

"Ah, no, I didn't," I said, surprise racing through me. Of course, if he was from a local grave, I might have known the person.

"We'll get an I.D. on him and see if it matches any of the recent graves that have been violated."

"That's a good idea," I said, nodding, because, well, what else could he do?

"Althea." Chief Thomas straightened and met my eyes. "I'm going to have to take you in for questioning. I'm sorry. I have to follow procedures here. But I'd like to ask a favor of you, and if you honor it, I'll do my best to stay openminded and work with you instead of against you."

"Why is that, if you don't mind me asking, Chief?" Luna smiled gently at him, and I felt a light brush of her charming magick over my skin. I knew she was softening up the chief to get answers from him. "Most would completely ignore what we know. Why are you willing to listen?"

"Because I've seen what you two can do. I know there's more that happens around us than I can explain.

And sometimes I think you have two choices in life – you can fight what is in front of your face, or you can invite it in and make friends with it. I've been involved in too many situations now that I can't explain away by any normal reasoning. It doesn't make me comfortable. Hell, I'm not happy about any of it. But I will give you ladies credit here – you've always tried to do what is right. I don't think you've always gone about it in the best of ways…"

Both Luna and Chief Thomas turned to look at me.

"Hey! I'm still learning."

"But I *do* think you really are trying to help. And if I have to deal with something beyond the realm of which I understand or care to think too deeply about, I'm going to use the tools at my disposal now."

"So I'm a tool now?" I glared at him.

"You're definitely a tool," Rafe whispered over my shoulder, and I almost whirled on him before reminding myself that Chief Thomas couldn't see him.

Luna's mouth quirked a smile, but she said nothing.

"Yes, Althea. You and Luna are tools to solve this. So, while we are off the record and I don't have you down at the station, tell me what you think this is, and I will do my best to keep an open mind."

"Here's what we think." Luna took over. "We think this is the work of a fairly new necromancer who has a maniacal sense of urgency. And we think it is a female doing this."

"A…" Chief Thomas squeezed the bridge of his nose. "A necromancer? And what is that?"

"They stuff souls in recently deceased bodies and make them come alive again," I said.

"That's the gist of it, yes," Luna said. "But it's more intricate than that. I think you have a woman on your hands who is new to learning her powers, has a sense of urgency on what she's trying to accomplish, and I think she will keep going until she gets what she wants."

"What do you think she wants?" Chief Thomas looked down at the body. "A zombie army?"

"These aren't zombies," I said, trying to help with my new brand of knowledge.

"What's the difference? Walking dead are…walking dead, aren't they?"

"A zombie can infect other people and it becomes kind of like a plague sweeping across the city as people get infected. This is a one-by-one situation. The witch doing this is summoning souls and plopping them into bodies. The problem is, she doesn't have as fresh a body as she needs, so the soul can only do so much maneuvering before body parts fall off and the corpse collapses."

"Ewwww," I breathed, and Chief Thomas looked at me, a smile hovering around his eyes.

"I'll admit, I'm with Althea on that. Ew."

"This is what we think. I wish I could profile more for you, but between us we could only get the sense of urgency and the fact she is female."

"How do I stop this?"

"You won't. We will." Luna shrugged at the chief's hard stare.

"I don't think you should be interfering with police matters."

"Okay." Luna shrugged again. "Best of luck to you then. I'm going back to bed. Oh, wait, I guess not. I'll have to open the shop."

"Wait, okay, I'm sorry. I'm not trying to kick you out of this. If this is really what's happening…" Chief Thomas looked down at the body and back up at us. "Then I will need your help in finding out what is going on and keeping it quiet or Tequila Key will go nuts. I just…you're going to have to give me a bit to wrap my head around this."

"I understand. We want to help," said Luna.

"Do we?" I asked her. Because I really didn't. I'd seen enough decomposed flesh for the rest of my life.

"Yes, Althea, we do. Because this will keep happening until she is caught."

"And that's a bad thing why? I mean, the people are already dead, right? It's not like she's killing someone," I protested.

"Grave robbing is illegal," Chief Thomas pointed out.

"Althea." Luna used her stern voice. "If she does not get what she wants from robbing graves, she will build up to the point where she takes a live human, kills them, and then puts the soul she wants in the body of the person she just murdered. Do you want that on your hands?"

"No," I said. "I really don't. I didn't know that is what would happen. I didn't know what a necromancer was before tonight."

"Neither did I," Chief Thomas said, sighing, "And I really wish that I didn't. Luna, do you think that is where this is headed? Why?"

"Because I suspect she's trying to bring back someone

she lost. The feelings here are raw. Grief is a hell of a motivator."

"Ohhhh," I said, as it dawned on me. "So we are looking for someone who wants to bring someone back to life."

"It's one way necromancers will use their power. Others are more insidious, like trying to control a town, or raise demons so they can bring dark magick into the world in a very real and corporeal form. But I don't sense that type of magick here. Did you, Althea?"

"No, not really. I felt like it was a woman who desperately wanted to be loved. Or accepted. Or something. There was like just an overwhelming feeling of need and urgency to it all. I'm sorry, I wish I could give more. But I'm still learning all this too."

"Okay." Chief Thomas blew out a breath. "Officially, I have to bring you in for questioning. We're going to do this all by the book. I'll have my guys come out and collect the body, and we'll do an identification on him. From there, well, we'll continue the investigation on our part. And you'll do yours. We keep each other in the loop, got it?"

"Yes, sir." I nodded, my stomach flipping at the thought of being brought in for questioning.

"I'll take Hank with me," Luna said, wrapping an arm around my shoulders. "Everything's going to be okay. I promise."

"We'll figure this out. We're a team, like it or not," Chief Thomas growled as he stomped away, pulling his phone from his pocket.

"Great, lovely to work with you," I shouted after him, and he shook his head at me.

"Don't poke the bear, Althea. He's being as fair as he can be in the situation."

"Fine. I know. I'm grouchy."

"What's new? Maybe you need to buy one of those sex toys from that new shop down the road that has the inflatable women in the window," Rafe said at my ear, and then disappeared before I could round on him and blast him with any spell I could think of.

"Wait." I paused and turned to Luna. "We have a new sex shop?"

"We can maybe stop there after you get back from the station."

Chapter Eight

CHIEF THOMAS WAS KIND ENOUGH to let me take a quick shower and tug a maxi dress on while he photographed the scene outside. Though I wasn't certain it was actually a crime scene, as no criminal activity had happened there, I understood his need to document everything.

I piled a few of Luna's protection crystal necklaces around my neck and tucked a gris-gris bag from Miss Elva in my bra. That was about all I could do about that, I thought, and looked down at where Hank had followed me into my bedroom.

"Buddy, you're with Luna at the shop today. I'll meet you over there." Crouching, I scooped him up and carried him downstairs with me to face what came next.

"All set? When is your first reading?" Luna asked, taking Hank from my arms and kissing his head.

"I have my first reading at nine. All the contact infor-mation is in my day planner on my desk. Can you reschedule for me? Offer a discount?"

"No problem. I'll throw in one of my gift baskets too. I'll just clear your day in case…well, we'll see how it goes."

"Probably for the best, I guess." Annoyance raced through me at having to reschedule. I might be flighty in some areas of my life, but I was a professional when it came to my work. I hated to cancel, but in this instance, I really had no choice.

"You call me as soon as you are out, okay? I'll be working magick on my end."

Luna hugged me, and I knew she was imparting protection spells on me because I could feel the wash of her magick brush over me like a cool, calming river.

"Althea, my guys are here. If you can just unlock your side gate so they can handle the scene, we'll clean up the body. We can keep your house locked up, and then I'll have someone lock the gate when they leave?"

"Okay, thank you," I said, dashing outside and unlocking my side gate. After making sure my back door was secure, I grabbed a toy for Hank – a cactus stuffed toy today – and snagged my purse from where I'd left it on the kitchen counter. "I think I'm all set. Thanks for giving me time to get ready."

"No problem. I truly don't think you have anything to do with this. But unfortunately, now you're involved. We've got to do these steps."

"I understand," I said, and then paused on the front porch where several policemen rolled out yellow crime scene tape in front of my house while my neighbors almost broke their necks trying to see what was happening.

"You've got to be kidding me. The whole town will be talking about me!"

"Um, yeah. I didn't think about that," Chief Thomas said, striding over to talk to his guys, who quickly rolled the yellow tape back up and put it in the truck. Nevertheless, the damage was done, as I could see more than one cell phone pointed in my direction.

"Lovely."

"It's too late. You know how this town is. Brace for the rumor storm to start. It's going to be a busy day at the shop," Luna said, glancing down at her outfit and grimacing. She'd probably just realized how'd she'd look on all those cell phone pictures circulating around town at the moment. "It's best I head out. I'll bring Miss Elva in to help later. Just call me immediately after questioning, okay? I love you." Pressing a kiss to my cheek, she dashed off with Hank in her arms and zipped away in her Mini before anyone else could take photos of her.

"My reputation is ruined. Again," I told Chief Thomas when he walked back over to me, gesturing to where all my neighbors were openly filming us now. "The whole town will think I did something bad."

"Isn't that the usual for you?"

"My, my, aren't we bitchy in the morning, Chief Thomas?" I glared up at him, hands on my hips.

He squeezed the bridge of his nose again. "Sorry. I just meant you're no stranger to people talking about you. From the outside, it seems like you handle it pretty well. Like water rolling off a duck's back. I didn't think something like this would shake you so much."

"Well, I'm glad I at least give the impression of keeping my cool," I murmured, walking to where my beach cruiser was locked to my porch. "But I'll admit, being the topic of conversation for the town isn't always a particular favorite pastime of mine."

"I'm letting you follow me to the station instead of putting you in the police car," Chief Thomas said, looking around at the neighbors. "Hopefully that will stem some of the gossip."

"Oh, aren't you an optimistic one? There's no stopping gossip in a small town. By noon I'll have murdered ten people and have buried treasure in my backyard."

"At least it won't be a boring day."

"I'm beginning to crave boring." Sighing, I threw a leg over my bike and pushed off, waving brightly to the neighbors as I passed them, smiling and trying to look as normal as possible. In all likelihood I probably looked like a cheerful killer clown biking away from a crime scene, but it was the best I could do on two hours of sleep. On the plus side, I didn't have a boyfriend to have to try to explain this to – so that was something.

My phone buzzed in my purse, and I pulled my bike to the side of the road, grabbing it and putting it on speaker when I saw it was Beau. Continuing to bike while holding the phone, I kept the smile plastered on my face.

"Althea, did you murder someone?"

"And good morning to you, my lovely Beau. To what do I owe the pleasure of this very early morning phone call? Don't you need your beauty rest to pick up all those hot men at night?"

"Well, at least you sound cheerful."

"I'm not cheerful. I'm trying to smile at everyone on the sidewalk like I didn't murder someone, but I fear I'm overselling it."

"Likely. Smiling at people is not your natural state."

"Good point," I said, and dropped the smile, returning to my usual of nodding at people as I rode past.

"What happened?"

I gave Beau the quick rundown as I pulled into the parking lot of the little police station located on the main strip of Tequila Key. Of course, the station had to be located directly across from the coffee shop, and I could already see people turned to the window to watch me. Who were these people getting coffee this early in the morning? Shouldn't they be at home hitting the snooze button on their alarm? Probably early-morning joggers. I shuddered at the thought. What did that say about me that I was more scared of the thought of an early-morning run than I was of a dead body knocking on my window? Best not to examine that too closely, I thought, as I locked my bike to the rack and walked into the police station.

True to his word, Chief Thomas led me through questioning, with another detective on hand to ask his own questions. We'd agreed ahead of time that we would go with the story of Hank having found the body on the beach, and left out the part about it walking into my backdoor. Once questioning was complete, I was free to go with the promise to not leave town and to keep my cell phone on. The second detective didn't say much, but I didn't like the look on his face when I answered the questions about how I found the body. Nevertheless, I was free to leave much more quickly than I had thought, and left the station with a desperate need for caffeine.

Eying the coffee shop, I tried to decide if it was worth the risk of gossip to go inside for my caffeine fix or wait until I got to work. The thing with small towns was that sometimes it was best to confront things head on. If I didn't go into the coffee shop and act normal, I'd be raising even more suspicion.

Sighing, I crossed the road and pushed the door open. The silence that fell over the shop when I walked in said everything I needed to know.

"I didn't murder anyone," I announced to the coffee shop, and I saw more than a few mouths drop open in surprise. "So you can just stop whatever gossip you're trying to start."

There, that should shut everyone up for a moment, I decided, and made my way to the counter to place my order. Though I'd promised myself I would stick with just coffee, because I didn't need the extra calories of something much more delicious and loaded with sugar, I got sidetracked by the display of cinnamon rolls in the pastry container.

"I'll have a triple mocha latte and a cinnamon roll, please," I ordered, instantly forgetting my promise to myself to take it easy on the sweets. I mean, if you can't order a cinnamon roll after a dead body knocks at your door, when can you?

My order arrived quickly, the barista giving me strong side-eye game the whole time, and I turned to leave only to run into Missy Sue, my client from earlier this week.

"Althea!" Missy Sue's eyes were bright with excitement, and I knew there was nothing she loved more than being the first to have the scoop on good gossip. "What in the world is going on? Why did you just tell the whole coffee shop you aren't a murderer?"

"Don't act like you haven't heard the rumors."

"What rumors?" Missy Sue blinked her heavily made-up eyes at me, all beguiling and nice, and I realized that she must sneak most of her gossip from people by playing innocent or dumb, whichever suited the moment. But I'd worked with her long enough now to know that while she may have been silly at times, she definitely wasn't stupid.

"You tell me," I said, moving to sit at a table so I could enjoy my cinnamon bun. Knowing me, I'd drop it on the way to my shop. Since I didn't immediately have to rush to my next client, I decided to linger and hear what Missy Sue had to say.

"Well, I'm not one to gossip …" Missy Sue said, pulling out a chair and plopping down across from me.

Right.

"Mmhmm, go on. Gossip anyway," I said, biting into my roll and enjoying that first rush of cinnamon sweetness.

"But I did hear a few things this morning about a crime scene tape in front of your house and you being arrested for murder."

"Not true. As you can see with your own eyes," I said, holding up the hand with my cinnamon bun in it, "See? No cuffs. And, no cuff marks either."

"Well, you know how ridiculous the gossips of this town are," Missy Sue sniffed, and then leaned in for the kill. "So tell me what really happened."

I debated this silently for a moment, not wanting to interrupt the nirvana of my pastry enjoyment. Police records were public, so whether I liked it or not, the story would be out soon enough.

"Hank found a dead body on my beach this morning when I let him out for his morning potty."

"No!" Missy Sue gasped and bounced in her seat, excitement crossing her face. "Did you know who it was? What did the body look like?"

"Not all there. This wasn't a recent death."

"Ohhhhhh, wow, okay." Missy Sue nodded. "So, do you think it is, like, the grave robber we talked about then?"

"It might be the case. If so, they must not have wanted the body."

"Hmm. But why your beach? That seems an odd place to deposit a body."

I seized the chance to control the narrative. "Obviously, someone has a vendetta against me. It's not uncommon. Being in my profession attracts all types of people." I leveled a look at Missy Sue, but my meaning was lost on her.

"Oh, that's crazy! The grave robber is targeting you. I wonder why."

"Who is to say? Have you heard anything else about them?" I deliberately didn't say that I thought the robber was a woman.

"Nope. Just that they always seem to manage to get through security. Though there's a new guy in town." Missy Sue widened her eyes and tilted her head several times to indicate a man reading his phone at the table in the corner. "A long-term renter. Just showed up. Soooo… "

"Right. So we're thinking anyone new in town is here to rob graves?" I studied the guy, who, while not looking particularly pleasant, also didn't look like a grave robber. That being said, I wasn't really sure what a grave robber looked like.

"I mean, it certainly couldn't be one of the locals." Missy Sue narrowed her eyes at me again. "Could it?"

"No, Missy Sue, I did not rob any graves. I have to get to work," I said, sighing and standing up. At that moment, the door opened and Theodore Whittier – also known as A Thorn in My Side – barged through the door.

"Of course you'd be here drinking coffee after murdering someone," Theodore all but shouted at me, looking like a busted can of biscuits in his too-tight pants and pressed shirt.

"She didn't murder anyone," Missy Sue piped up, and the people's heads swiveled like they were watching a ping-pong match.

"And you would know this how?"

"Because she's sitting right here. You can't arrest someone for finding a dead body."

"It's always something with you, Althea," Theodore said as I made my way to leave.

I advanced on him, forcing him to step back or risk me barreling him over, and never broke eye contact with him.

"Careful what you accuse me of, Theo." I smiled at him and he visibly blanched. "We know some of your secrets."

"That's…just…you can't…" Theodore blustered as I pushed past him and opened the door that chimed merrily.

"I can. Watch your mouth before I sue you for slander."

With that out of the way, I hopped on my bike and whistled the whole way to my shop.

Chapter Nine

"DID you really clear my schedule for the whole day?" I asked Luna, sitting on a low-slung chair in her back room and watching while she mixed ingredients for an arthritis tonic that was quite popular with the older folks in Tequila Key.

"I did," Luna said, and shot Hank a look as he stuck his nose into one of her baskets beneath the table.

Without having to say a word, Hank backed off and retreated to come paw at my leg. I pulled him up in my lap and he cuddled in, quickly falling asleep. I realized it had been a busy night for him as well. "A day off! How exciting. Except I guess we're going after this grave robber, aren't we?"

"You've guessed correctly."

"Do we have to?" I know I sounded like a whiny child, but I was on two hours of sleep, and really wasn't in the mood to uncover any more dead and rotting bodies. I was at the limit for the day, as far as I was concerned. Hell, for the month that is. I shuddered when I thought about the shriveled bits of flesh on the corpse found in my backyard.

"Yes, we have to. We don't know the reasons behind why any of this is happening. I know I just told you that there might be a vendetta against you this morning to get you to call the police, but…"

"You did?"

"Duh, of course. Calling the police was the right move. However, I can't get a read on what is going on here yet, so we actually can't rule out someone targeting you. For whatever reason."

"Oh. That's *fun*. I like that. That's really what I need-ed." I nodded vigorously before inhaling the rest of my mocha.

"Like it's what I needed? In case you haven't noticed, I don't particularly care for my best friend being targeted. Not to mention that work is insane right now. Have you seen my online orders?" Luna nodded to the empty jars and bottles lined up on her worktable. "I'm so behind that I'm thinking I'll need to bring in part-time help. It's not like I want to take the day off either."

"Can I help? How about this – I'll help you for the morning and we'll see if we can get you back up to speed. Then we'll call Chief Thomas this afternoon and see if he has any other information. If so, we'll go from there?"

"We could run some diagnostic spells and see if we can track this witch," Luna mused.

"First let's deal with your backlog. You'll be more focused to handle any spells if that's off your mind." Luna was a perfectionist, so I knew it had to bother her to have delays on her shipping. After all, reputation was every-thing in our business.

"Fair enough. Okay then. Let's focus. I can't have you running any magick, because, well…"

"That's fine. I get it. And with zero sleep, I'd likely turn us all into snakes or something."

"Exactly. But you can help me fill the bottles. I've already mixed several batches that had been basking in the moonlight last night and are ready for bottling. Here's the tool I use." Luna went into her pantry and brought out three silver bowls, and then looked at me and back down at the bowls. "You know what? Let's do one bowl at a time."

"Best not to mix things up," I agreed, and she smiled at me.

I'd feel horrible if I put the wrong cream in the wrong jar, so I was more than happy to keep things simple. Luna put on some lilting Celtic music in the background, and we had a pleasant and uneventful morning of packaging tonics, creams, and potions and being comfortable in silence around each other. Hank snored blissfully on the chair, and by lunchtime, I was half-convinced that nothing untoward had happened that morning. Luna had decided to close her side of the shop this morning, and we had seen more than one person pull up before reading the closed sign and leaving. Half would be customers, and the other half were looking to gossip. Luna didn't seem to mind being closed, so I didn't press her on it. By the time we'd finished with her orders, the tension seemed to have eased visibly from her face.

"I'm feeling so much better," Luna admitted, wiping

her hands on her apron before untying it and hanging it on a hook by her workbench. "I didn't realize how much that was bothering me."

"If things get really busy, you know I'm more than happy to help. Maybe instead of going to Lucky's for a drink, we stay after and get this done once a week so you don't get too far behind again?"

"You don't mind doing that?"

"Luna, I would do anything for you. It's silly to let your orders build up like this without asking for help. I'm here. Use me."

"We really do need to get you to that sex shop." Luna winked, and then we both looked up as Miss Elva breezed in the front door in a screaming-red caftan dusted with gold sequins.

"I thought you locked the door?" I asked.

"I did." Luna narrowed her eyes at Miss Elva. "Someone is using her magick."

"Locks don't stop Miss Elva," Miss Elva laughed. "Get in the car, we've got a situation."

"You have a car?" I stood and peered out the front window where a blush-pink Land Rover was parked at the curb. "A pink one at that?"

"My baby loves me." Miss Elva gave a cheeky smile. "And it comes in handy."

"The Flamingo King bought you a car?" Luna asked.

"He did, because he knows I deserve the best."

"Buying her love," Rafe sniffed, appearing over Miss Elva's shoulder.

"I won't say no to a gift." Miss Elva shrugged, ignoring Rafe.

"What's the situation, Miss Elva? I'm hungry."

"I've got snacks in the car. Let's roll. Trace needs us," Miss Elva said.

"Trace? What's wrong? Is he hurt?" I asked, my stomach flipping and tying itself in knots. I already had Hank's leash on him and my purse on my shoulder before Luna had even locked up her backroom.

"He's...not hurt. But he's not in a good space."

"Gee, that's a lot of info, thanks, Miss Elva," I said, already pulling my phone out to check. I didn't have any messages from Trace, which was odd, as I thought he would call me if he was in trouble. What was she playing at?

I settled into the backseat with Hank while Luna took the front, and braced myself when Miss Elva hauled herself into the driver's seat and hit the accelerator like Nieman Marcus was having a seventy-five percent off sale.

"What are we dealing with?" Luna asked. She'd grabbed her large burnished leather tote bag, which I knew carried an endless supply of all things magickal, and I straightened as I realized we might be heading into a magickal battle. My stomach growled.

"I have snacks for you." Miss Elva glanced over her shoulder as she careened down the street, "They're in that bag. Here, let me..." She reached back with one arm.

"No, no, no." I yanked the bag from the floor. "Eyes on the road, Miss Elva."

"Please," Luna begged.

"Funyuns?" I pulled out a bag. "And Gardetto's? Is this like road trip food?"

"Well, we're kind of on a road trip, aren't we?"

"Are we going to Trace's house?"

"Yes."

"That's like…six minutes away. Not much of a road trip," I pointed out.

"Not much time to snack either then, is it?" Miss Elva shot me a glare.

"Right, got it." I dug into the Gardetto's, eyeing the Funyuns suspiciously. I knew people loved those things, but could never seem to get myself to try them.

I'd only gotten through a few handfuls of my pretzels by the time we'd pulled to a screeching stop in front of Trace's little house. It was hard to eat due to the fear threatening to choke me as Miss Elva blatantly ran more than a few stop signs.

"I'm driving us home," Luna decided, getting out on shaky legs.

"Snacks?" I offered Luna my bag weakly and she just shook her head at me.

"He says come straight through to the back," Miss Elva said.

"Why is he texting you and not me?"

"Probably because you kicked him to the curb and he doesn't trust you. Or, more likely, I'm the one he needs the help from." Miss Elva shrugged.

"I did not kick him to the curb. There was no curb kicking. We mutually took a break."

"Althea, just focus," Luna said, digging in her bag and pulling out a small bottle.

We stopped at Trace's front door, offering a perfunctory knock before trooping into his house. A small two-bedroom, one-bathroom house, it was set up essentially in a square shape, with the bedrooms at the front and a hallway leading to the kitchen and living area that opened to a neat backyard.

Trace stood, his back to us, staring out the sliding glass door to his backyard. I dropped the leash, and Hank beelined for Trace, who immediately bent and scooped him into his arms. It was when Hank let out a low growl that fear trickled through me. Hank rarely growled, and this was twice in one day.

"Oh no," I breathed.

"Oh yes," Trace said, turning his head to meet my eyes. "We've got a problem."

I came to stand by Trace and looked out into his back-yard. Surrounded by a high fence, the backyard had been turned into a dude-zone with a comfy outdoor couch, a small firepit, a massive grill, and a beanbag toss. A corpse wheeled erratically around his garden, banging its fists on the fence and tearing down one of the hanging plants I had put up for Trace. I winced as a chunk of flesh dropped from his hand to the ground.

"Is he…is he talking?" Luna asked, tilting her head as the body did another erratic shuffle across the yard.

Turning, he zeroed in on us.

"He is, though it's been hard to make out his words," Trace said, turning back to look at the destruction in his yard. I had to say, he was taking this all in stride. Points in his favor, I guess.

"How did you find him?"

"I came home from the boat for food. Was going to eat it outside and…well, almost opened the door to this."

"Yikes."

"Yikes indeed. So I called Miss Elva, and here we are."

I wanted to wheel on him and ask why not me? Why not call me first? But then I realized I hadn't called him in the middle of the night when I was scared either. That was something to ruminate on at another time.

"Trace, can I just slide this open a smidge? I'd like to see if I can understand what he is trying to communicate," Luna asked, gesturing to his door.

"I'm thinking that's not a great idea. I don't want to become a zombie, Luna."

"These aren't zombies. As you can tell, he has very little control. We just need to speak to the spirit to see if we can get any clues on who put him in this body."

"Right." Trace ran a hand through his blond hair, and I could feel the tension rippling over him. Momentarily distracted by the muscles in his arms, I felt my insides go liquid. Maybe I did need to go visit that sex shop, I thought, and tore my gaze and my libido away from Trace and back to the walking death in the backyard.

"Okay, just a smidge. Let's hear what he is saying." Luna nudged the door and we all leaned over as the corpse drew closer, his one eye focused on me.

"Schnaccchshhsss."

"Huh, not getting that. You need to speak up," Miss Elva called.

"Scccchnnnnanncksss!" the corpse screeched, banging its fist on the window in front of me. I jumped, startled, shaking the Gardetto's bag in my hand.

"What's that? Be clearer," Miss Elva ordered.

"Snaaaacks!" the corpse shrieked, raising its arms to the sky before toppling over backward on its head.

"Oh. Oops," I said, glancing down at my snack bag while the other three looked at me and collectively shook their heads. "Hey! How was I supposed to know the corpse wanted snacks?"

Chapter Ten

A SPIRIT POPPED out of the body in the shape of an overweight and slightly unkempt man. His eyes zeroed in on my bag of Gardetto's again, and then he looked down at his hands. A mournful expression crossed his face, and he lifted puppy-dog eyes back to mine.

"I just wanted to taste food one more time," the spirit sighed.

"Quick, Rafe, Rosita. See if you can get him to stay with us." Miss Elva directed the two ghosts who had surprisingly kept in the background during this whole ordeal.

"I'd hardly call that food," Luna said, eying the bag in my hand with distaste.

"I'm just going to put these down," I said, turning and putting the bag on the coffee table behind me.

Since it seemed like the threat of danger had passed, as there was no spirit to operate the body, we decided to slide the door open and step outside. Three women surrounded the spirit, while Trace looked at us oddly and stared down at the body slumped on the patio, his expression hard as granite.

"I'm sorry you didn't get your snacks," Miss Elva said, opening the conversation with the spirit. "We couldn't understand what you were saying or of course we would have offered you some. We're not rude like that."

"I appreciate that." The spirit nodded, his tone as gray as a soggy, stormy morning. "But it's to be expected. Nothing ever seems to work out in my favor."

"That's a tough cross to bear, I agree," Miss Elva said. "Since you're here and we can see you, do you mind if we ask you a few questions?"

"Oh, you're not dead, are you?" A mild form of surprise rippled across the spirit's face as he zeroed in on the three of us. "But these two are."

"Yes, this is Rosita and Rafe. And you are?" Miss Elva said, introducing her two ghosts.

"I'm Earl. Nice to meet you."

"Hi, Earl. Can you tell us where you were when this happened?" Luna asked.

"I…" Confusion caused Earl to pause for a while as he tried to think it through. From my understanding, time worked differently in the spirit realm, so I wondered if he even knew how long he'd been over here or where he'd been before. "Hmmm. I was on the other side, that's for sure. And then I got pulled over."

"Pulled over? How does that work?"

"Well, part of it was my fault. I was kind of testing my boundaries. Hovering too close to the line, so to speak. I guess I wanted to see what would happen if I could make it back to this world."

"So, kind of like a whirlpool? You got too close and it sucked you in?"

"No, I wish. Then I'd come here all the time. Lots of fun to be had here. I was definitely pulled in by…hmm… something? No, someone. That's right." Earl snapped his fingers. "She shoved me in this body. I have to admit, it was pretty painful."

"She?" I asked.

"Painful how?" Miss Elva asked.

"Where were you?" Luna asked.

Trace, to his credit, did not interrupt us. Instead, he held Hank in his arms and leaned back against the sliding glass door to let us do our thing. There was something to be said for a man who accepted us and didn't try to take charge of a situation when he saw someone else was better equipped to handle it.

"Um, wow, so…yes, she," Earl said, nodding to me. "And it was painful because you don't feel the same when you are in spirit form. Like your senses aren't the same physically. So being slammed into a human body that isn't mine and one that is…decidedly unhealthy…well, it is not a great experience."

I didn't point out that Earl didn't look like he'd been particularly healthy before he died, because who was I to comment on someone's weight? I was the one who had just been fist deep in a bag of snacks, and frankly, it wasn't good practice to assume overweight people were also unhealthy. I slid a glance to Miss Elva. The woman was large, curvaceous, and physically stronger than Luna and I put together. Others would say she was fat, but she was healthy as could be. So, no, I would withhold my judgment of Earl. Hopefully, someone would do the same for me.

I snapped back to attention when Luna nudged me.

"I'm real sorry to hear that. I have to imagine it was pretty painful. The body you were put in was not a good choice for a fine specimen such as yourself," Miss Elva said, and Earl puffed his chest out, much to my amusement and Rafe's dismay. I don't know how Miss Elva did it, but she could charm the pants off a dead man. Or men, it seemed, as I saw Rafe's face go thunderous.

"It *was* a poor choice. I deserve better," Earl agreed.

"You deserve death, you stinking mongrel!" Rafe seethed, and Earl reared back, turning on him.

"How dare you? You smelly, ugly, lame excuse for a man. Walking around in your pirate costume," Earl shot back.

"Cos...costume?" Rafe sputtered. "This is not a costume. I *am* a pirate. A real one. Unlike the likes of you...what were you? An accountant? You don't know the first thing about being a man. Or how to pirate and pillage. How to show a woman a good time!"

"It's like watching two potatoes argue with each other," Rosita decided, and the rest of us wisely kept our comments to ourselves. "I wouldn't bet money on either of these two knowing the first thing about how to pleasure a woman."

"That's preposterous. Of course I know how to give pleasure," Earl scoffed, turning to Rosita. "I studied manuals. I know where the woman's pleasure button is."

"Did he just say *pleasure button*?" I whispered to Luna, and Trace perked up at my words.

"I must be missing something good," he said.

"Fill ya in shortly, it's heating up."

"Manuals? You studied manuals? What about actual women? As in letting them instruct and lead you so that you know how to give them pleasure?" Rosita demanded.

"Um…" If a ghost could blush, Earl would.

"Oh." Miss Elva nodded, understanding dawning. "You've never been with a woman, have you? That's okay, honey. Some of us are late bloomers is all."

"A virgin!" Rafe cackled, and Earl turned on him, ready to spew.

"It's not like you had many women jumping into your arms either, Rafe. At least not that you didn't have to pay for." Rosita raised an eyebrow at Rafe.

"Ohhh, not such a big guy, are you now? Maybe the pirate costume was off-putting for the women?" Earl smiled at Rafe, who all but vibrated with rage.

"Children. That's enough," Miss Elva said, her eyes on Rafe, who looked ready to explode. "We need to get some more information from Earl."

But the damage was done. Rafe, unable to control himself – shocking, I know – screeched and lunged for Earl. As soon as his hands closed on the other ghost, Earl disappeared in an instant, and we were left with a confused and angry Rafe floating in front of us.

"Well, that is not the ideal result we were looking for," Luna declared, crossing her arms and looking down her nose at Rafe.

"Rafe, have you considered anger management class-es?" I asked.

"Rafe, really," rebuked Miss Elva, "You could have

handled that better. We needed to get information from Earl. How are we supposed to know who is doing this if you keep acting this way? Now we'll be dealing with more spirits when the next body arrives. And the next spirit might be even more handsome and exotic than you. Keep that in mind," Miss Elva warned, and Rafe's face fell.

"You don't love me anymore. You just want something new all the time. I thought you were my lovemountain, but now I don't know anymore." With that, Rafe winked away, probably to cry and hug his comfort blankie.

"How in the world do you put up with that every day?" I asked Miss Elva.

"He's much calmer when it's just us. He's a little prone to dramatics when he has an audience."

A little? I mouthed to Luna, who pressed her lips together and shook her head slightly at me.

"So what did we learn?" she asked.

"We can confirm it is a woman doing this. And that she is pulling unwilling spirits through," I said.

"Well, not totally unwilling. He was flirting with the line. So not as strong magick as we are thinking," Luna mused, waving a hand in front of her face to diffuse the smell of the body next to us. Like that was really going to help.

"How so?" I asked, going to stand by Trace and pet Hank's head.

"If a spirit has gone really far into the realm or ascended to the next level, it takes much stronger magick to pull them back to this world. The ones that are still dancing with the line, not quite ready to move on, those can bounce over pretty easily," Miss Elva explained.

"Like Rafe."

"Right. He still wanted to play here."

"So did I," Rosita admitted. "Humans are endlessly fascinating as far as I am concerned."

"Then we are looking for a newer witch? Or one new to her powers?"

"Yes, my bet is someone new to the game. And a triggering event made her brush up on her skills or led her to desperately learn something. She's in trial mode. It's going to ramp up," Miss Elva agreed.

"Which means…" Trace looked at me and then back down at the corpse.

"Which means more graves will be robbed until we figure out who is doing this."

"Oh, great," Trace said, and I looked at him in agreement.

"Right? This is just *so* fun."

"Is there any way we can do a tracing spell?" Luna looked to Miss Elva, who had come to stand over the body, eyeing the corpse in disgust.

"We'd have to pick the body over to see if she left any of her hair or something like that as evidence," Miss Elva said, looking up at Luna and myself.

"Nope." I shook my head. "Do not look at me. I am not touching that thing."

"I…I have to agree with Althea. I can't see us figuring out what DNA may be what on this." Miss Elva nodded.

"Should we go to the cemetery? Could we learn anything there?" I asked, and Miss Elva nodded thoughtfully.

"I don't think that's a bad idea, Althea. Maybe we could do a reenactment spell."

"What's that?" Trace asked.

"Depending on how long it has been since a crime has been done, sometimes we are able to bring up kind of like a visual replay of what happened," Luna supplied.

"Like watching a security tape for evidence?"

"Basically. But, you know, with magick. And it unfolds in front of you."

"Weird. But cool," Trace decided.

"It can be really helpful. It's just a matter of all of the elements falling into place correctly."

"I say we give it a go. I have to admit, I don't think I have the stomach for finding any more rotting bodies." The Gardetto's were already rolling in my tummy, and I was certain that standing in that backyard for a moment longer was going to produce some unsavory results from me. "I'll just be inside."

I stepped inside and took the first clear breath I'd had in moments when a knock sounded at the door. Curious, I walked through the house, and my stomach churned even more when I saw who was on the other side. Opening the door, I grimaced.

"Althea? Well, isn't this interesting?"

"Chief Thomas. What are you doing here?"

"I'd ask the same of you."

With that, I turned and heaved the contents of my stomach into the bushes outside Trace's door.

Chapter Eleven

IT WAS a hectic few moments before I was able to sit quietly on the couch as Chief Thomas had instructed, where we waited until he could get a handle on things. I sipped the Sprite Trace had given me, grateful that the sliding glass door had been closed and the worst of the smell had dissipated. This was definitely starting to add up to one of my least favorite days, and I'd had some doozies of late. It was just so…icky.

"You doing okay?" Trace asked, his arm thrown lightly behind me on the couch.

Despite everything between us, I leaned into him just a little. He didn't pull back, so I think we both needed the comfort. "Sorry about your bushes."

"It's okay. I'll hose them down when this is done."

"I'm also sorry you have to deal with all of this," I said, looking up at Trace, and then remembering I probably had gross breath and turned my face away again.

"It sounds like you've already had to deal with this once today. Why didn't you call me?"

"It was like three in the morning, Trace."

"And? You called those two."

"I know. But they're magick. And this falls in their realm. Also, I can't lean on you for everything. I have to learn to handle some of this on my own."

"I thought we were friends?" Trace asked, his voice wounded.

I realized I'd hurt him with my words. "We *are* friends. And sometimes friends have to be understanding. Remember, you didn't call me either when you found this body. You called Miss Elva."

"Fair point," Trace said after a pause. "I guess I was thinking same as you. Magick."

"But I am magick as well. So I would be a logical person to call." I realized I probably wasn't helping this situation.

"Well, so maybe we are both just flexing our independence a bit."

"Sure, I guess. It's weird," I admitted, turning once more to glance at him. "This transition is weird."

"It is. But we promised each other we'd navigate it. I don't want to lose you, Althea."

"I don't want to lose you either, Trace," I said, squeezing his leg.

"I hate to interrupt this very touching moment, but could we maybe discuss the dead body on your doorstep? You know...if you can fit it in your schedule?" Chief Thomas asked, his arms crossed over his uniformed chest.

"Oh, sure, sorry," I said, glancing around to see everyone in the room staring at us. How long had they been listening in?

"So. This is an interesting development," Chief Thomas began, his eyes on me. "I believe we'd promised each other we'd keep each other in the loop?"

"We've only been here like fifteen minutes. Time was crucial and we were going to call you, I promise," I said.

"Why was time crucial?"

"The body was still walking about. We wanted to talk to the spirit and try to get information," Miss Elva supplied.

"Right, and you realize this is increasingly tough for me to believe? I am trying with you guys, I am *really* trying to suspend disbelief. But I also have to look at the facts. And, well, the facts aren't looking very favorable for you."

"Chief Thomas? How did you know to come here? Did Trace call you?" Luna asked, changing the flow of the conversation. She also made a damn good point.

"Yes, how did you know?" I asked.

"We received an anonymous phone call. Luckily, I was the one to answer it or you'd have an officer on the scene and who knows where this would have gone."

"An anonymous tip? Was it to your cell phone or the land line at the station?" Luna asked.

"Land line. I already thought about that."

"Too bad." Luna pursed her lips and sighed.

"I'm sorry about almost throwing up on you," I said, looking up at Chief Thomas. "As you can see, I'm not super happy to be around these dead bodies."

"I do see that. Which is why I'm willing to give you some leeway."

"I highly doubt we'd conjure a dead body up, then call

an anonymous tip in to frame ourselves," Miss Elva pointed out. "Especially if this one can't handle being around the dead."

"I can handle it some. It's just been…like way over my threshold for a day."

"You have a threshold of death you can handle?" Chief Thomas zeroed in on me.

"Yes, apparently it's two dead bodies in a day. Threshold reached."

"I suppose. But to your point, Miss Elva, it would also be quite smart to call yourself in and arrange this situation if you wanted to warn me off of your scent," Chief Thomas said.

My mouth dropped open. "Wow, diabolical. I never would have thought of that."

"No, *you* wouldn't have." Chief Thomas dismissed me and looked at the other two.

"Hey! I'm smart!" I complained, glaring up at the chief.

"Chief, would it help if you could review the security footage from my camera?" Trace interrupted us before I got into a petty argument.

"You have cameras? That would be great, actually," Chief Thomas said, and Trace stood to go to his laptop, which was sitting on his breakfast bar.

Opening it up, he clicked on the camera app and we all waited in silence as he loaded the recent video.

The three women stayed sitting while the men bent over the laptop, and I let my eyes wander around the room. It was a typical bachelor pad with more eye to comfort than style, but I noticed he'd kept the drum fish photo I'd given him framed over his couch. It was something, at least, to feel like I was still part of Trace's life.

I realized in that moment how much I missed seeing him every day – spending time together laughing over coffee, or going on an early morning dive before he took clients out. I understood that this transition would take time for us to ease back into a friends routine, but now my feelings were all confused and swirling about inside. It was like…I wanted him as more than a friend but also wanted space. How did I even begin to navigate that?

"You look like you're going to throw up again," Luna said, leaning over to study my face. I felt a cooling brush of her magick roll through me and knew she was doing a silent soothing spell on me. It helped, but not for what she was thinking it was for.

"Just having some uncomfortable life thoughts," I said.

"Such as?"

"How can I be so contradictory? I want one thing and then I want the other. I flip back and forth and can never seem to make up my mind. How do I know what's right?" Both women's eyes darted to Trace and then back to me.

"That's because you're a Gemini child. I swear, it's a constant battle of which personality is going to win out each day," Miss Elva said. "You have some growing up to do. You need to make peace with who and what you are before you can know what you want elsewhere."

"I thought I *was* at peace with who I am. I love my job, I don't hide my work, and I have a fun side hobby I very much enjoy," I protested.

"Oh, Althea. There's so much more of your magick

you're not tapping into. Your mother even told you so," Luna said.

My mother, Abagail Rose, psychic to the stars, was still on her world tour where she bounced from one fabulous place to the next and gave readings to people who could afford to buy small countries. I was constantly receiving gift packages on my doorstep peppered with exotic spices or tiles from Morocco. My father, true to his passion, would send music, and I had a growing collection of international collections to play in the background at work. I missed my parents, but I didn't think they'd be home any time soon. They were having too much fun exploring, and I certainly didn't blame them. Tequila Key could grow a little constricting at times.

This would be one of those times, I thought, as I eyed the dead body outside the door. Hank came over and pawed at me until I pulled him into my lap for a cuddle. He'd had a stressful day as well, and I wanted to make sure he knew I was there for him.

"Well, I'll be damned," Chief Thomas swore.

I tuned back into the situation in the living room. On the small laptop screen a video played on a loop. Because it was in black-and-white, it appeared like a scary movie to me – reminding me a bit of *The Blair Witch Project* movie – and even though I had seen the dead body moving with my own eyes, I still gasped as a hand shot over the top of the fence and the body heaved itself over in jerky movements. It landed with a plop in Trace's backyard and then stood, before beginning its erratic movements around the yard – arms held high – and its mouth open in what looked like a silent scream on camera.

"I'm sorry, but that's horrifying," I said, looking away from the screen. I could not handle scary movies. I just could not. My dreams after watching a scary movie were less than pleasant, and I certainly didn't need any more fuel for nightmares. I already suspected tonight was going to be a tricky night for sleep.

"I thought y'all were used to this stuff." Chief Thomas looked over at me.

"I think the term 'used to' is stretching it. We've dealt with it a few times. That doesn't mean we like it. Do you show up at a murder scene and not get upset?" Luna asked.

"No, they still bother me. It's sad to see a life end violently," Chief Thomas admitted.

"And, we're exactly the same, child. It's not our practice to deal in dark magick or blood magick, so we prefer not to deal with dead bodies at all. This is equally as horrifying to us, frankly, if not more so because we know how bad this can get. Right now, we're trying to think three steps ahead so as to stop this person, while you're over here cleaning up the messes. And if you want our help, I don't suggest you make assumptions or patronize us," Miss Elva huffed, smoothing the sleeve of her caftan.

"Down, girl." I winked at Miss Elva, patting Hank's belly.

"Well, I don't need my reputation being besmirched by some man saying I hang out with dead bodies all day," Miss Elva sniffed, and my brain was still tripping over her use of the word *besmirched* before Trace interrupted us.

"If you're thinking three steps ahead, what do you need to do next?"

"I'd like it if we could have access to the cemetery

tonight," Luna asked, "We might be able to gather some information or even better, intercept the witch doing this."

"Witch?" Chief Thomas sighed and scrubbed a hand over his face.

"Or maybe we could do it tomorrow night? You know…when we're well rested and alert?" I asked, hopeful for some semblance of sleep tonight.

"Reenactments spells are time sensitive, Althea," Luna whispered.

"Yeah, but…" I sighed and looked down at Hank in my lap. "Maybe we let Chief Thomas stake out the cemetery tonight and then we go tomorrow night."

"Oh for goddess' sake, get yourself an espresso and woman up. It's time for the ovary gang to take charge of this here murder case." Miss Elva heaved herself up and stood, hands on hips, looking like she was ready for a rampage.

I was more ready for a nap.

Ovary gang? Trace mouthed at me while Chief Thomas stood there, his mouth hanging open, as we'd finally managed to shock him.

"You heard me, Trace. Ovary gang. The women are always the ones who have to handle the tough shit. Show me any man stronger than a woman and I'll show you a fool."

Trace looked at me, and I gave him a very subtle head shake. He wisely closed his mouth.

"What time would you like access to the cemetery tonight?" Chief Thomas finally asked.

Miss Elva nodded her approval at him. "I think around midnight should be fine. It will give Althea enough time to sneak a nap in, and you can finish cleaning up this mess in Trace's backyard. Plus, the witching hour is typically a good time for spells."

"Spells." Chief Thomas nodded. "Right. Magick. Witches. And walking dead bodies. Maybe I have finally gone off the deep end."

"You and me both, Chief Thomas, you and me both," I said.

Chapter Twelve

WE HAD AGREED to meet at my house at ten to go over some of the magick ahead of time. I was really the only one who needed to refresh myself on magick, as the other two kept up their magick practice religiously. For me, it was more like my yoga practice. I'd promise myself I'd start a new routine – dive headfirst in and go at it for about a week – and then I'd get distracted by something else and forget about yoga until the next time I'd give it a go. Though, in the case of magick, I'd be wise to actually stick to the practice because from my estimation it didn't look like weird shit was about to stop happening to me. I wouldn't always be able to rely on Luna or Miss Elva as a backup.

"When did life get so complicated?" I asked Hank, who had just finished downing his dinner like he'd never see food again.

Smart dog, I thought. *I'd better do the same.* I popped a frozen pizza in the oven and set the timer, then stepped outside to settle on my outdoor couch to throw the ball for

Hank. I'd managed a few hours of sleep after Chief Thomas had shooed us out of Trace's house to deal with the body, and we'd all decided that we needed some rest before our next adventure.

Adventure, I laughed to myself. When I'd hear people talking about having an adventure, I always thought it was stuff like hiking Machu Pichu or rock climbing. I did not consider hanging out in a cemetery at midnight trying to catch a grave-robbing witch an adventure. At the very least, not in my top ten choices of adventure options.

A knock sounded at my door and had Hank scrambling, as his favorite thing in the world was to announce to the neighborhood that he was the true owner of this house and none should enter without his assent.

"Cash!" I said, shock racing through me as I pulled the door open. "Well, this is a surprise."

Cash, looking as handsome and perfect as he always did, leaned in the doorway and smiled his devastating smile at me. Tall, broad-shouldered, with muscles that ran straight down his chest to…well, let's just say to a place I have enjoyed visiting. He looked cool and confident in his light linen button-down and loose khaki pants.

"Hey, beautiful. I've missed you." Cash stepped in and pulled me in for a deep kiss.

Should I have stopped him? Maybe. But it was hard to remember my commitment to taking space for myself when all my hormones had sprung to attention and were singing a chorus of hallelujahs as Cash's hands wandered down my sides to cup my bottom.

"I've missed you, too," I said, breaking the kiss to catch my breath. Quickly, I peered past him to make sure no dead bodies wandered the street, then tugged him inside to slam the door behind him. "I haven't heard from you in a bit."

"Is that a problem?" Cash asked, moving across my living space as though he owned it. "I thought you had wanted to keep things loose after the Bahamas. I believe those were your exact words."

That doesn't mean he had to stop calling, I thought, miffed.

"Sure, I just was commenting on not having heard from you. It wasn't a criticism. An observation," I supplied, and moved to the fridge to get him a beer.

"Mmhmm," Cash said.

A wise man, he refrained from commenting further and potentially getting castrated and instead bent to pet Hank, who circled him enthusiastically.

"Beer?"

"Sure, thanks. I'm just in for a few days as I need to go over the recent renovations to two of our developments here. I thought I'd take a chance and surprise you."

"As in you were looking for a booty call," I said, and then winced at my tone. In my head, I'd thought I'd gone for light and teasing, but it sounded accusatory even to me.

"Whoa, no, I never assume a woman will put out. What's up with you, Althea?" Cash asked, a wounded look on his handsome face, and I sighed, turning as the timer on my oven sounded for the pizza.

"I'm sorry. I'm having a bad day and I did not get a great sleep. Let's start over. I'm happy to see you and how are you since the last time I saw you?"

"I'm good. Work has been slammed, and I'm really

tired," Cash admitted, and I turned, just now noticing the dark circles ringing his eyes. "It's all good stuff, so no complaints. It's just a lot to juggle right now."

"Have you considered bringing on more help?"

"I have. But even then, it's the teaching and training. That is time consuming in itself. And then I have to doublecheck two sets of work – mine and someone else's."

"Oh, right. That sounds annoying."

"It is. I'll get there when I find the right person, but it's not happening right now. Too many of these projects are such high level that they need delicate handling."

My face flamed as I thought about my own delicates that he had handled, and I was grateful my back was turned as I sliced my pizza.

"Pizza?" I asked, turning to him.

"Sure, I'll have a slice. You're eating late. Is that due to your bad day?"

I thought about how to answer him. This had been a particularly difficult area for our relationship, and one of the reasons Cash and I had ultimately never ended up working out. While our chemistry was strong and we genuinely liked each other, Cash still deeply struggled with accepting my magick, no matter how many times he'd now borne witness to it.

Remembering Miss Elva's comments about accepting who I was, I turned with two plates in my hand and slid him one, while settling next to him on a stool at the breakfast bar. "Yes, it's been quite a day. And it isn't over yet. I have to go back out tonight to try to catch a grave robber."

Cash's hand paused halfway to his mouth, the slice of

pizza hanging midair while he digested what I'd just said. "Okay then. Um, that sounds dangerous."

"We'll see." I quickly filled him in on everything else, and by the time I was done he'd put the slice of pizza down and reached for his beer instead.

"That's...hmmm," Cash said, and took a long pull from his beer bottle.

"It's a lot, I get it. I can't say this is my favorite thing to deal with either. But it literally showed up at my doorstep, and I have the magick and the friends to deal with it. So here I am."

"Here you are," Cash agreed.

"Still tough for you, huh?" I asked, biting into my pizza and trying to ignore the resentment that burned in my stomach. If I didn't care what he thought about my life, then his judgments wouldn't matter. One thing was for certain – I was not going to try to hide who or what I was.

"It is. I'm getting better with it. But then when I think I have it handled, something new pops up. Zombies, huh?" Cash took another sip. "That's..."

"Some shit," I finished for him. "But also, not zombies. Spirits stuffed inside dead bodies by a newer witch who is not used to her powers."

"Right. Got it."

"I'll admit it's freaked me out a bit too. But this is my life. Hopefully it gets less crazy at some point."

"That doesn't seem to be the current trajectory."

"No, it does not. Which I'll have to learn to deal with then. Either way, I've decided to spend some time dating myself." Eeek. I hadn't meant to say that last part out loud as, honestly, I just sounded ridiculous to my own self.

"Is that right?"

"Yes, I think I need some time to adjust to all these new changes and also figure out what it is I want out of life."

"That's not necessarily a bad thing to do. Being happy on your own is something many people haven't learned to do. I even struggle with it. But I'm so busy lately that I don't have much time to think of anything else."

"Maybe you also need to date yourself for a while until you figure out work and life balance."

"Hmm, maybe so." Cash smiled and finished off his beer before standing. "I should go. It sounds like you have an eventful evening ahead and I don't want to kill your vibe or anything like that."

"Thanks for stopping by, Cash. It's good to see you," I said, turning on my seat and hugging his waist.

Bending, he pressed a kiss to the top of my head. "Be safe tonight. Call me if you need help."

"I will."

"Oh, and Althea?" Cash asked as he reached the door. "Let me know if you need a hand...with anything...while you're dating yourself."

Oh my, I thought, and turned back to my pizza, my hormones screaming. Duly noted.

Chapter Thirteen

"WE JUST SAW Cash on his way out." Miss Elva barreled in the door before I even had time to switch gears. "That man is fine."

"I'm aware," I said, cranky once again and not sure what to do about it. If I didn't want to be in a relationship, I surely couldn't get upset about a man who couldn't accept my lifestyle, right? And yet here I was. Queen of Contradictions.

"Maybe you sent him off too soon. It seems like he could've taken care of that mood of yours if you'd let him," Miss Elva observed, putting a huge, black sparkly tote bag on my counter.

I surveyed her apparel with interest. Black leather leggings, black sparkle Converse, and a black sequined tunic that screamed Graveyard Chic if that was even a thing. If the moonlight hit her just right, she'd glimmer like a disco ball.

"I can't. I'm taking 'me' time, remember? Plus, I

scared him off with the whole walking dead commentary and all."

"Child, you tell him this stuff?"

"I have to, right? You just lectured me on accepting myself. Doesn't that mean the people in my life need to as well?"

"Sure, if they're going to be there long-term. But your playthings? They don't need to know all of your inner goddess secrets. Some things are best kept under wrap."

"I think Althea was struggling with deciding whether Cash could ever move out of the toybox and into the house." Luna smiled at me. She looked ready for an evening of tromping around the graveyard in jeans, tennis shoes, and an olive-green button-down shirt. I was the only one not wearing pants, and now I realized that could potentially impede me if I needed to run.

"Keep him in the toybox. He's a fun diversion, but can be put away as needed." Miss Elva nodded, bending to pet Hank.

"Okay, yes. Let's just…I don't want to think about men right now. I'm going to run up and change into something more suitable for the cemetery. Make yourselves at home, I'll be right down."

I hustled upstairs, determined to ignore all thoughts of men, and instead focus on the task ahead of me. It was just…thoughts about sexy men were way more fun than thoughts about walking dead bodies. My mind wanted to go where it wanted to go and I certainly didn't blame it.

Sighing, I changed into simple black leggings and a loose Grateful Dead T-shirt, and piled my hair into a bun on top of my head.

"I like the shirt." Luna laughed when I came back downstairs. "Very apropos for our evening."

"Could use some sparkles." Miss Elva eyed my shirt. "But I like the dancing bears."

"Thanks. It's my father's. Hopefully it brings us good energy tonight. He's always been a lucky man."

"He's lucky because he found your mom."

"They're both awesome." I smiled, my heart tugging again as I thought about them. "I really miss them."

"Maybe you should take a vacation and go visit them. Where are they now?"

"Bali. I think?"

"That sounds fun. I bet good diving," Miss Elva said.

"Sure, I'll start looking at tickets now. You guys go handle this. I'm out," I said.

"Nice try. Okay, Althea, let's go sit and talk about what we plan to do tonight." Luna shooed us all outside and soon we were seated on my back patio, a candle flickering on my table, and Hank at the ready with a ball in his mouth.

"Okay, I'm ready. Hit me with it," I said, tossing the ball that Hank dropped in my lap. It was an unconscious movement by this time, as I did it so many hours a day.

"Do you understand the purpose of a reenactment spell?" Luna asked.

"It seems fairly self-explanatory, no? Just kind of like replaying the security tapes that Trace had, but in a magickal way."

"Correct. But we're also asking the spirits to do the reenacting for us. There has to be a give and take here. Because of the energy we are using, spirits will come in and basically playact the scene for us. If we're lucky, we'll get the actual spirit that was involved in the incident. If not, we'll get a stand-in."

"But how will that work for the witch who is still living? If a spirit does a stand-in for her, how will we know who she is?"

"Ever heard of costumes, honey? The spirits pull the person on. Like a skin cloak."

"Ew," I breathed, the visual not particularly pleasant.

"It will be just like looking at the person doing it," Luna hastily amended before I went too far down the road of thinking about skin cloaks.

"Well, let's hope this is helpful. Then we can wrap this up and get back to normal life," I said, tossing the ball again for Hank.

"It's not that simple, but yes, I agree. So, we'll need a few ingredients…"

"Salt," I offered, remembering how Luna had used salt to cast a circle in the past.

Both Luna and Miss Elva leveled pitying eyes upon me like it was my first day of school and I was proud I'd known the answer to roll call.

"Yes, Althea. We use salt every time we cast a circle. However, I'm talking about ingredients used in our spell casting." Luna, ever the patient one, patted my knee.

Turning to each other, Miss Elva and Luna commenced to argue for the next ten minutes about the worthiness of particular ingredients until my eyes began to glaze over and I'd wished I hadn't carb-loaded with my choice of pizza for dinner. I could happily go upstairs and curl right up in bed.

"Althea," Luna said.

"Right, ginger." I snapped to attention and nodded sagely at both of them.

"Ginger?" Miss Elva narrowed her eyes at me.

"I mean, ginseng. Right? Boosts memory? Or is it rosemary? I can never remember. Get it? Haha."

Luna at least gave me the courtesy of a laugh while Miss Elva shot me a death glare.

"We will use rosemary, and she's not wrong about the ginseng, I suppose." Luna pursed her lips and considered it, and I straightened my shoulders feeling like I'd actually contributed to the conversation.

"Best not to muck it up with too many extras. I like to keep things clean and simple," Miss Elva said. It was my turn to eye the glittery disco ball of Miss Elva balefully.

"My spells, that is." Miss Elva met my look dead-on.

"And definitely not with her men," Rafe said.

"Oh, I think simple is too high of praise for you, Rafe." I smiled sweetly at the ghost, who made an unbecoming gesture at me and flitted off as Hank bounded over to him.

"We'll stick with the rosemary then. Let's go over the plan and give Althea a general idea of how long this will take and what to expect." Luna hurried on, doing her best to keep us on track.

"Yes, I don't want to make any mistakes like in the past." I held up my hand as though making a pledge. "Honestly. I really would like to enact one spell smoothly where we get the desired outcomes."

"Good, because I don't know that I can handle another ghost in my house," Miss Elva said.

"She's got all the ghost she needs in me!" Rafe shouted

from the other side of the garden, where Hank continued to stalk him.

"I swear…that man's ego. He talks a big game. But according to my ladies at the brothel…" Rosita made a deflating noise and held her finger up straight before letting it collapse.

"Lies!" Rafe shrieked, and Hank gave chase, delighted at the enthusiasm. "No! Devil beast! Back off!"

I laughed at the pandemonium that ensued, happy to have someone else to keep Hank entertained for a bit, and turned back to Luna. "Okay, let's do this. Salt for the circle. Then what?"

"Then you invoke the elements. We'll all stand inside the circle and stay inside the circle until the spell has run its course. Why do we do that, Althea?" Luna asked.

"Because the circle protects from negative energies."

"Correct. Now, once we've called the circle, Miss Elva and I will begin the spell. It shouldn't take long to enact, but we have no idea how long the actual spell will run for."

"Why is that?" I asked.

"Because we can't know how long it took for the new witch to run her spell. It could have been done in ten minutes or it could take an hour. The reenactment spell will run its course through to the end of the scene, so to speak." Luna dug in her purse and pulled out a box of mints. "Let's hope it doesn't take an hour or we'll all get tired."

"Wait, we'd just stand in one spot for an hour?"

"Unless you care to step out of the circle?"

"No, no. I got it. Okay, cast circle, mix ingredients,

don't interrupt the two of you while you call the spell, and then wait to see what happens."

"Pretty much. Though I think it is high time you start adding your magick to the mix," Miss Elva said.

"How do I do that?"

"You have to focus on that core element. Remember, we discussed this? When you close your eyes and go within? There's a flow of energy. It's kind of like turning a faucet on and off." Luna mimicked the turning of a faucet on. "You want to find that and then direct the flow toward the spell with the intention to aid the magick on to work in the intended way."

"I can try," I said.

"Just don't turn the faucet all the way on. You have a lot of power and we don't need a firehose exploding the spell," Miss Elva said.

"Um, sure, no problem," I said. I mean, it was absolutely a problem, but I wasn't about to let them see that.

"Then we're all set. Althea, you'll leave Hank here, I presume? It's safest for him." Luna looked to where Hank had cornered Rafe against the fence.

"Yes, absolutely. Hank!" I called, and Hank bounced away from Rafe, running over to me with a doggy grin wide on his face.

"I can stay here with this love bucket," Rosita crooned. She loved Hank about as much as I did, but mainly because he harassed Rafe constantly.

"Thanks, Rosita. That would be great."

And with that, we all trooped inside to get ready to run a magick spell to hunt down a grave-robbing witch.

It seemed the idea of living a calm life had sailed out the window.

Chapter Fourteen

"LET the record note that I can think of many more enjoyable ways to spend my evening," I said. We were nearing the cemetery and anxiety slid through me in a hot trickle that pooled in my stomach.

"Like what? Did you finally go to that new sex shop?" Miss Elva slapped her knee and laughed as she barreled her Land Rover toward the gates of the cemetery, where Chief Thomas's car was parked. "I know it's not with a man since you sent that fine piece of meat out of your front door instead of up your staircase."

"I was thinking more along the lines of rum and a reality show marathon," I grumbled.

"You're getting boring in your old age, Althea. Getting older is supposed to free your inhibitions, not give you more. Isn't it time you embraced that?" Miss Elva shot me a glance over her shoulder, and I swear my heart screeched as she continued to drive at a breakneck speed.

"Being a passenger in your car is about as lowered as my inhibitions can get. Will you slow down?" I all but shouted before Miss Elva hit the brakes hard enough that we skidded along the dirt road and shuddered to a stop about three feet from Chief Thomas, who regarded us with a look of horror on his face. Had there been any intruders about to sneak into the cemetery, I was certain Miss Elva's roughshod approach would have warned them away – that and every forest critter within twenty miles.

"We really need to discuss your driving skills. When was the last time you even owned a car?" Luna asked Miss Elva.

"Um…that's a good question, honey. I think maybe twenty years ago? If not longer."

"I'm driving home," Luna said, and gingerly reached for the door handle.

"Child, how am I going to get better if you don't let me practice?"

"What are you practicing for? The Indy 500?" I asked, hopping from the car, my legs shaky beneath me. It would have been dramatic to drop to my knees and kiss the ground, but I was working on being *less* dramatic. Instead, I leaned against the car and drew in some deep breaths to calm myself while Chief Thomas approached.

"Ladies. Might I suggest you follow the rules of the road before I regret ever allowing you to be a part of this investigation?" His face was grim beneath his hat, and I didn't blame him in the slightest for the harshness of his tone.

"Talk to this one. I'm riding home in your car instead," I said, and pointed at Miss Elva.

"I wasn't aware you knew how to drive," Chief Thomas said. "Do you have a license?"

"Of course I do, honey. What? You think Miss Elva isn't a law-abiding citizen?" Miss Elva put her hands on her hips and stared down Chief Thomas.

We all looked away at her question, nobody daring to be the one to take the bait.

"Well, if we had someone who was about to sneak into the cemetery, I suspect they've been well warned away. So, the best I can do is give you an hour here while I sit outside the gate. Just…no funny stuff."

"What is that supposed to mean?" Miss Elva, hands still on hips, glared at him.

"I think what's he's trying to politely say is that if we can do our best not to make the situation worse, he'd greatly appreciate it," Luna said.

Chief Thomas nodded curtly in her direction. "Luna is correct. Do your thing and all that. But just…let's not make things worse. I really hate writing up reports where I can't accurately explain what actually happened."

"You just tell the truth." Miss Elva shrugged, her shoulder glittering in the moonlight. "I don't see the issue there."

"Because not everyone believes in your truth."

"That's not my problem." Miss Elva turned and pulled her purse from the car. Miss Elva, despite her many eccentricities, was also a goldmine for inspirational quotes.

Chief Thomas just turned and looked at me. I shrugged, because what else was there to say? Miss Elva was technically correct – her truth was the truth as it happened – and if people didn't want to believe in magick, ghosts, or spells, then there wasn't much else she could do. It didn't matter how many times you presented someone with facts. If they didn't want to believe, there was no changing their mind.

"Is there anything that I should be prepared for tonight?" Chief Thomas asked.

"We plan to run a reenactment spell. Which, essentially, is going to be like playing a security tape backwards if we do it right. Don't be alarmed if you see some light or spectral energy. It's normal," Luna said.

"Right, normal." Chief Thomas drew out the word *normal* as he shook his head slightly.

"Well, *our* kind of normal. Hopefully we'll get some information on what's happening."

"Might I suggest you put in actual security cameras at the cemetery? That way you wouldn't need our magick to help you do an instant replay." Miss Elva poked her head out of the car, where she was digging in her purse.

"We tried that. They keep getting disabled."

"That's too bad." Miss Elva shook her head sadly. "Unfortunately, nothing is fool-proof."

"I appreciate your help this evening." Chief Thomas gave Miss Elva a curt nod and she beamed at him in return.

"That's very kind of you. We don't often get thanked in our work, as some of the stuff we do can dredge up deep emotions for people and they forget to be grateful for our help."

I pressed my lips together at that. I was certain Chief Thomas wasn't entirely grateful for the proverbial thorn in his side that we were. Nevertheless, he'd learned to work through the pain.

"Right. Well, have at it, ladies. You have one hour."

"You hear that, Althea? We have to be fast." Miss Elva elbowed past me, a glittery disco ball of purpose, and strode blissfully through the wrought iron gates of the cemetery.

"Don't worry about her, Althea. We'll just do as we discussed." Luna patted my arm and, with one last glance at Chief Thomas, who sighed and leaned against the hood of his cruiser, I followed her into the graveyard.

As cemeteries went, I suppose it was fairly standard. A high cement wall surrounded the cemetery, largely to protect from any massive flooding if a tropical storm blew through. Gravestones of all ages and types were scattered about amidst larger above-ground mausoleums. A few trees and bushes were tucked around the gravestones, mainly for aesthetics, I presumed, but managed to look dark and sinister in the moonlight. I mean, sure, if I looked at a tree at night outside of a cemetery, it wouldn't bother me. But, clutter a few gravestones underneath one, and suddenly it seemed like a perfect hiding place for zombies who were looking for a snack.

And I had no interest in being that snack.

"This is the spot," Miss Elva called from across the graveyard.

It wasn't hard to spot her and I beelined toward the glitter. Who would have thought my safety blanket would be draped in sequins and could swear like a truck driver?

"Oh, wow," I said. I stopped next to where Miss Elva stood over a large hole that had been dug in the ground near what looked to be a fairly new gravestone.

"This here took some effort. She had to dig for a while

to get to the body. It's not like it is one of those above-ground graves," Miss Elva said.

"No, it's not. That's a lot of manpower," Luna agreed.

"Could she have magicked it?" I asked.

"I suppose there's a spell for pretty much everything. It's hard to say. We don't really know how long she was out here," Luna said, unpacking her bag and turning in a circle to assess our surroundings.

"I think here's the best spot for a circle." Miss Elva indicated a dirt patch next to the grave and just steps off the walkway.

"We might have to crowd in a bit." Luna looked around at the other gravestones, eyeing the distance, and I knew she didn't want to include the graves in her circle.

"That's fine. I don't mind." I really didn't. The closer I was to these two, the less chance I had of being nabbed. Like by a hand reaching out of that dark and dank dirt hole in front of me. I shivered and stepped closer to Luna.

"Let's get started then." Miss Elva grabbed a jar of salt and motioned us over so she could create the perimeter circle around us.

Luna bent and placed crystals on the directional points of the circle, and I stood there and did nothing, doing my best not to mess with their process. Once they'd completed the circle, Luna brought out a small silver bowl and both she and Miss Elva began to add various ingredients. How they knew what was what in the soft light of the moon, I did not know. Biting my tongue – I was learning that my best contribution these days, was to not interfere with the professionals – I waited until they deemed their spell to be properly mixed.

"I believe we are ready," Luna said, looking up and tucking a strand of blonde hair back that had dared to come loose from her topknot. It was as disheveled as I'd ever seen her, which meant this was serious.

"Okay, I'm ready." I nodded vigorously.

"Remember what we've discussed? Your power will greatly add to this spell. You just have to turn the faucet on and let it flow," Miss Elva said, reaching for my hand. Luna bent and placed the bowl in the middle of our circle and then stood to reach for us. We stood, hands locked together, and all looked down to the silver bowl at our feet.

"We'll begin the spell now," Luna said.

"We have to be fast. We don't know how much time we'll need. Be fast," Miss Elva urged and Luna nodded. "Got that, Althea? Fast."

"I got it," I bit out.

"Element of Air, I call upon you," Luna began, facing east, and continued around the circle, turning us with her as she invoked the elements. Once the circle was cast, she looked up and met my eyes. "It's time."

I took that to mean she wanted my power.

"We need to go fast," Miss Elva urged, "These reenactment spells can take ages."

I closed my eyes and sought to find that inner well of power that Luna insisted resided inside of me. As Luna began her spell work, I found my power.

"Oh spirits of nigh,
We ask you try!
A crime held here,
Must reappear.
Show us as you can,

The events that once ran.
For the truth must prevail,
And to you, we do avail."

When her words finished, I released my power and it raced through me, pouring out into the circle, and I squeaked as the silver bowl lit from within and shot a beam of light straight to the stars. Luna and Miss Elva gasped.

"Althea! No! Too much!" Luna shouted, and I whirled as spirits sprung from the grave at our feet.

Chapter Fifteen

"WHAT'S HAPPENING? What did I do?" I exclaimed as several spirits poured from the dirt hole in front of us and whipped up into a frenzied tornado above our heads before separating out and dropping to the earth.

"Too much power," Luna said, digging rapidly into her purse. "We need to slow it down."

"What do you mean, slow it down?"

"Child, you've gone and put this reenactment spell on fast forward," Miss Elva said, her lips pursed as she studied the spirit, who was rapidly shifting from an ethereal being to what looked like a real person crouching next to the grave.

"I did? I didn't know I could do that. I didn't even know that was an option," I protested.

"Well, it is. And you did it."

"But you kept telling me to go fast. That this has to be fast. I just did what you asked, didn't I? I reached for my power and opened the faucet. I didn't know that I could dose it out in like a small trickle or whatever… " I watched as the woman at our feet, her head turned away from us, rapidly mixed ingredients in a bowl and cast a circle.

"It's a faucet, Althea." Miss Elva turned and looked at me, holding her hand up and mimicking a turning motion. "You understand the concept, yes?"

"Of course I know what a faucet is."

The woman on the ground stood and began to chant. I couldn't hear what she was saying. It was like watching a rabid mime as she lifted her hands to the air and made fast jerky motions.

"Well, what happens when you turn the faucet on all the way?" Miss Elva demanded.

"Okay, I've had just about enough of this. You didn't prepare me appropriately," I said. "Just pay attention. We need to move so we can see her face."

I moved to step out of the circle so I could see the woman's face, and Miss Elva jerked me back so hard that a spasm of pain ran up my arm.

"Do. Not. Step. Out. Of. This. Circle."

If there was ever a time I was scared of Miss Elva, now was that time. Her face was dead serious and she held my eyes until I nodded once.

"I can't believe she is trying to step out of the circle. When we are in a graveyard full of mixed spirits just waiting for a chance to pounce. What does she think is gonna happen? That the nice spirit is going to pop out and say hello? It's never the nice ones that come knocking on your door, remember that, honey."

"I wasn't thinking. Just…leave me be. I'm trying to

concentrate." I stuck my lip out, like a petulant child, and turned away from her to watch the scene all while Luna continued to grab ingredients from her bag.

There was something vaguely familiar about the way the woman moved, even if it was in fast forward, and I narrowed my eyes trying to catch a glimpse of her face as she moved around the grave, her head angled down, and continued to mutter her spell. Despite knowing the grave would have to be opened, I still gasped when dirt shot in the air and covered my head. When nothing hit my face, I glanced over to see Miss Elva biting back a smile.

"Sorry, it's much more real than I had anticipated," I admitted, realizing that the dirt was a part of the vision.

"Her face is painted. Kabuki-style makeup it looks like," Miss Elva said when the woman turned for a split second and then kept moving.

A coffin rose rapidly from the grave and landed on the grass next to the woman, who immediately crowbarred the top off and got to work. I was amazed at her strength but had to remind myself that it probably took a lot longer to get the top off than what I was actually seeing. By the time the body rose from the coffin, Luna was about ready to do a new spell.

"I'm just missing one ingredient. I don't know how to slow this down," Luna said, and I turned to look at her.

"It might not even be worth it at this point. It's almost over."

"I would be able to hear what they are saying, though." Luna was right. Everything was moving so fast it was impossible to tell or hear what words were being said.

"It's Snacks!" Miss Elva proclaimed, and we realized the body was our zombie buddy from Trace's house. His head rotated animatedly as the woman dropped to her knees and held up her hands to him, her shoulders shaking as she shouted to him.

"Yup, really would have been helpful to hear what she was saying," Miss Elva said.

"Yeah, yeah, I get it," I said, my shoulders slumping.

We watched as the woman stood and we all jumped as she slapped Snacks across the face and then stormed away, in the opposite direction from us. Snacks looked around in confusion and then lumbered off after her before disappearing from sight.

Silence greeted us and we all waited, holding our breath, to see if anything else would happen. When nothing did, I turned to look at Luna.

"Too late." Luna sighed and looked down at her hands full of ingredients.

"Can we run it again? Like a double replay? I promise not to put any energy in."

"No, you most certainly cannot. You can't test the spirits like that. We're lucky we even got that clear of a reenactment." Miss Elva shook her head sadly.

"I'm sorry, Althea. It's best we don't." Luna patted my arm.

"Should we chase after them? Maybe we'll learn something as they go." I turned and Miss Elva yanked my arm again.

"Ow! Stop doing that."

"Stop putting me at risk by almost stepping out of our safe zone. Let Luna close the circle," Miss Elva said.

"Oh. Right. My bad."

I waited as Luna thanked the spirits for their help and swiftly closed the circle. Finally, when Miss Elva gave me a small nod, I stepped away from the circle and took a shaky breath in.

"That was amazing!" Rafe chortled, zipping up and slapping his knee as he laughed. "It was like watching live theater. Or…kind of. But like…what were those stupid guys who ran about hitting people on your television? Black-and-white? Nuk nuk?"

"The Three Stooges?" I asked.

"Yes, kind of like one of those shows. All fast and zipping about. What great fun! And, it was good to see my mate Cameron again."

"Cameron? Who is Cameron?" I asked, eyeing Rafe and wondering if this was another one of his stories.

"Ah, Cameron. He was one of my shipmates. We plundered many a sea together. He was there when I died, you know," Rafe said, sweeping his arm out in front of me.

"Wait, where was Cameron?"

"Well, it's hard to say, but I think that – well, now that I think on it…" Rafe tapped a finger to his lips. "I think he was the one holding the gun on me when I died."

"Wait. No. Rafe. Focus on now for a second. Where was Cameron?"

"Oh, he was the spirit in the woman with the weird makeup on. He did a stand-up job if I must say so myself."

"He playacted the woman for us?" I asked.

"He did. And a great job he did. Didn't he?"

"Really lovely. Think you could have a little chat with

him and get more details on the woman he was playing?" Luna asked.

"I could…but…hmmm," Rafe continued to tap his finger on his lips until his features turned thunderous. "That traitor!"

"Excuse me? Who and what is a traitor now?"

"I'm finally remembering! Cameron is the one who killed me. Held me at gun point and robbed me. At Rosita's brothel of all places! Can you imagine being curled up in the arms of a woman? Recently sated from the throes of passion? Her whispering what an amazing lover I am? To only have the door kicked in and a gun held to your head? It's…oh, the tragedy of it all!" Rafe threw his arms in the air and let out a wail.

"Wait…you're saying this Cameron killed you? Your friend and shipmate?" I asked, narrowing my eyes at a hysterical Rafe, who raced to Miss Elva for comfort.

"Yes! That bastard! I shall find him and haunt him. I can only hope his death was even more painful than mine. Oh, my lovemountain! Can you believe I was taken in such a fashion?"

"It's a very distressing thing to hear, it is," Miss Elva agreed, and made cooing noises over Rafe.

"How can you believe this?" I exploded, throwing my hands in the air. "I swear every other week he has a different story on how he died."

"How. Dare. You." Rafe drew himself up and shot daggers at me with his eyes.

"Well? You pull me along on these sob stories and now I don't know what to believe!" I put my hands on my hips and glared right back at him.

"My lovemountain! This wench with bad taste in clothes dares to besmirch the story of my untimely demise. Will you allow such behavior?" Rafe begged of Miss Elva.

"Althea, be nice. Maybe it's hard to remember your death after you've died."

"Oh please, I suspect that's a pretty pivotal moment to remember." I glared at Rafe, not giving an inch.

"Perhaps he doesn't want to remember," Luna said softly, tugging my hand, and I realized she might be right. Rafe hadn't lived a kind life, and I suspected whatever retribution might have been visited upon him certainly hadn't been a nice way to go.

Considering, I tilted my head at him. "I guess the part of the story I'm having the most trouble with is where this woman you were with claimed you were an amazing lover."

"You! You! You insidious fat wench…like you would know anything about lovers! About giving love? You can't even keep a man!" Rafe worked himself into such a tizzy that he just poofed away and we were left in silence.

"Uh…sorry about that. I can't resist sometimes." I shrugged a shoulder.

"In all fairness, he's very rarely nice to you," Luna agreed.

"He was particularly dramatic tonight. He's been a bit moody these days. I think I need to spend more time with him." Miss Elva sighed. "You know how men are. They always need attention."

"Which is why I'm not dating for a while," I said, turning to look around the graveyard. "Men are just too much work."

"I'm sorry to hear that," a voice, only slightly slurred, whispered over my ear, and I shrieked as an arm wrapped around my waist. "Because I'd very much like for you to call me Daddy."

Chapter Sixteen

"GROSS!" I said, before bringing my elbow back to drive into a decidedly squishy and decidedly smelly gut. "Ewww, double gross."

I looked down at my elbow, covered in dried blood and bits of skin. The smell alone was something that I wouldn't discuss in polite company.

"Oh, yeah, baby," the zombie slurred in my ear, and I squeezed my eyes shut.

"Ewwwwwwwwww, get him off me!" I screeched.

"Just call me Daddy. Yes…ohhhh, that's what Daddy likes."

The zombie grabbed for my breast and I wrenched myself from his arms, digging my nails into his palms, and shrieking once more when a finger came off in my hand. Jumping away from him, I dropped the finger on the grass and ducked behind Miss Elva, working to control the heaves that threatened to deposit my dinner all over the pile of dirt at my feet.

The zombie just laughed and gyrated in front of us, grabbing himself between his legs.

"Now, this zombie sure has some real attitude, doesn't he?" Miss Elva shook her head and clucked her tongue.

"Not a zombie," Luna said automatically.

"Sure looks like one," I said.

"He'd have bitten and infected you by now if he was," Luna shot back.

"Fine. Either way, he's not a someone I particularly enjoy being around," I bit out as I struggled to calm my breathing.

"Oh, you think you're real fine, don't you, honey?" Miss Elva stepped forward and drew the zombie's gaze.

I didn't care if he wasn't a zombie. Looked like one. Acted like one. Smelled like one. Same difference in my book.

"Oh, you're a big one, ain't ya?" the zombie slurred, and at that I looked up, actually worried for the zombie now as Miss Elva's hands went to her hips.

"Excuse me?"

"You a big girl. I like 'em all shapes and flavors, though. You want to call me Daddy?" The zombie smiled and began to move toward Miss Elva. She reached in her purse and threw a little bag at him, which stopped him in his tracks. He seemed frozen, though his mouth was still capable of moving. "That's fine. You want to restrain me and do the nasty? That's fine by me, sugar. Just call me Daddy."

"I might actually be sick," I said.

"I knew a guy like him once. He always wanted to roleplay that daddy shit." Miss Elva shook her head sadly.

"Didn't work out. I'm not one to play power games like that. I like to be in charge. And I like the man who is with me to know he's getting *all* woman, you hear me?"

"Um." I wasn't sure who she was asking, exactly.

"But...but..." The zombie pouted. If someone whose lips were missing could pout. "The other one called me Daddy. I thought it was what you humans liked."

"Wait, what other one?" Luna stepped forward at that.

"The woman. The one who pulled me over the line. She was calling me Daddy. I just thought...I don't know. It's been so long since I've known the touch of a woman."

"What else did she say?" Luna asked.

"She ran when I tried to kiss her. Just like in my old life." The zombie hung his head sadly.

For a moment, I felt bad for him. Until I remembered him reaching for my breast.

"Well, you should ask before you take, then. Women don't like it when you force yourself on them," I said. "You should know better."

"I just...I just want a woman. Any woman. Please..." the zombie begged, but he was held tight by whatever spell Miss Elva had thrown at him.

"Can you tell us anything else about this woman? The one who you just saw?"

"She...so pretty..." The zombie's face went slack, and I saw a blur as the spirit vacated the body and hovered over it, looking sadly from the frozen corpse suspended in air and around him.

"Did I hear you making a move on my lovemountain?" Rafe zipped up and confronted the ghost.

"Wait, Rafe. We have some questions..." I said.

"How dare you?" Rafe attacked, and a whirlwind of blurring apparitions whipped around us until it stopped so suddenly that I blinked, staring up at the stars above my head.

"What just happened?" I asked.

"I defended my lovemountain's honor. Nobody may speak to her that way."

"Thank you, my love. You are my king," Miss Elva said.

"But…" I said, annoyed that Rafe had ruined our chance to talk to a spirit who might give us more clues on the witch who was doing this.

"Even better than that Flamingo King?" Rafe asked.

"Of course, honey, you are my spirit king." Miss Elva gave me a look and I pressed my lips together.

"That was…just… I think I might need a drink." Luna wrinkled her nose as she studied me. "And you may need a shower."

"What we need to do is find out how someone got in here when Chief Thomas was sitting right outside," Miss Elva said.

"Oh my gosh, you're right," I said, worry for the chief lancing through me. I mean, I wasn't a huge fan of the police, but he was one of the good ones. And goddess knows I'd seen some bad ones. Like the one who'd tried to kill me…

"Let's get out of here." Luna bent over and packed ingredients into her bag.

"What do we do with that body?"

Miss Elva walked over and said a few words over the body before tapping her finger once in the air. The body dropped to the ground like a marionette who'd lost his puppeteer.

"Do we have everything?" Miss Elva asked, looking around.

"I think so," I said.

"Come on, Rafe honey. Why don't you take me home and we can curl up together? You did such a fine job defending me tonight."

"He was very crude," Rafe sniffed, his nose in the air like he was suddenly a paragon of politeness.

"He was. Nobody should speak to a lady this way."

I thought she was being generous with the definition of a lady, but I supposed I wasn't exactly in the department to judge on that particular criteria. I scanned the graveyard as we hustled toward the gate, looking for any other surprises or fast-moving zombies. At this point, I didn't think much would shock me.

Except for when we walked out of the gates to see Chief Thomas lying on the ground. Yup. That was definitely a surprise.

"Chief Thomas!" Luna exclaimed.

I ran to his side and dropped to my knees, feeling for the whisper of a pulse at his neck. When I felt the flutter at my fingertips, I looked up and nodded at Miss Elva and Luna. "He's alive."

"Should we call the ambulance? Or take him in ourselves?"

"Will he get in trouble for being out here and helping us? I think he was technically violating the rules…" Miss Elva pointed out.

"Let's load him up and take him to Mathias," Luna

decided. "So long as nothing seems broken, I don't think it would be wrong to do so. I'll call Mathias right now."

Mathias, Luna's amazing boyfriend and physician, was well used to our unusual lifestyle and the ramifications that came with it. She was already holding up her phone so that Mathias could examine the chief through the video and determine if he should be moved or not. Once he was certain nothing was broken that we could see, he gave us the go ahead to bring Chief Thomas to his practice for examination.

The problem was – could we lift him?

"I think he'll fit in the back of the Land Rover best," Miss Elva decided. "If we lay those backseats down, he can stretch out real nicely."

"That makes the most sense," I said, and dug my hands in Chief Thomas's pockets for his car keys. He shifted and mumbled a bit, but didn't waken. "I've got his car keys. Should we just leave his gun on him?"

"I'm not touching it. I don't want my fingerprints on any police-issue weapon." Miss Elva shook her head. I noticed she didn't say she had a problem with her fingerprints being on any other weapon.

"I've laid the seats down," Luna said, rounding the back of the Land Rover and popping the back hatch open. "Mathias said we want to make sure to hold his head and neck stable if we can."

"I'll do that," Miss Elva said.

I didn't point out that Miss Elva was stronger than Luna and I combined and maybe she should take the brunt of Chief Thomas's weight. We didn't have time to get into an argument and I was actually worried that he wasn't waking up. I slid my hands under his back, grimacing as the rocks beneath him cut into my arms. Luna did the same with his legs, and on a count of three we lifted him. I gasped as he all but floated into the air.

"Are we that strong or did someone add a boost of magick?" I asked as we leisurely strolled to the car and gently deposited the chief in the back with very little fuss.

"I can't be doing too much manual labor now, you know. I might chip a nail," Miss Elva said, studying her glittery black nail polish.

"Okay, I'll lead the way," I said, excitement coursing through me at the thought of driving a police cruiser. I've always wanted to throw on the sirens and race through town.

"Uh-uh." Miss Elva put her hands on her hips. "Who says you get to drive the police car?"

"I do," I said, holding up the keys. "And you have to drive your car."

"Luna can drive my car." Miss Elva stuck out her bottom lip.

"I've seen how you drive. You are *not* getting control of this police car." I glared right back at her.

"I honestly don't think either of you are responsible enough to drive the police cruiser," Luna said, nipping the keys lightly from my hands before I could stop her.

"But...but..." I said.

"No time to argue." Luna was already in the front seat of the police car with a slightly maniacal grin on her face.

"That's not fair." Miss Elva turned to me. "This is your fault."

"It is not! You were the one who had to argue about it."

"I did not argue. I merely suggested that I be the one who drive the police car."

"And I suggested you weren't capable of doing so."

"And I…" We both jumped at a loud whoop from behind us.

"Ladies!" Luna's voice thundered over the bullhorn and we both slapped our hands over our ears. "That's enough!"

"What the hell?" Miss Elva actually stomped her foot.

"Get in the car. Now!" Luna shouted at us.

"Wow. I never knew she'd get so power-hungry," Miss Elva shook her head sadly as she climbed in the driver's seat of the Land Rover. "I tell you, Althea. Some people can't handle even the slightest bit of authority."

I bit my tongue as I buckled into the passenger seat and glanced back at Chief Thomas, who was now making moaning noises. I would lay bets that Miss Elva would be ten times more abusive of her power if we had let her drive the cruiser, though I couldn't exactly say that I wouldn't be too.

When Luna flipped the police lights on, I held my breath and waited for the siren. Instead, she drove demurely away, the lights flashing to give us some authority, but with enough restraint not to turn on the siren.

"I would have turned on the siren. Some people…I swear, they waste the best opportunities." Miss Elva clucked her tongue, and I slapped my hand on the dashboard as she peeled away from the cemetery gates.

"It's a damn shame," I agreed.

Chapter Seventeen

"WELL, she did run at least one stop sign," I pointed out as we pulled up to Mathias's practice.

The lights were glowing behind the windows, which meant he'd already arrived and was prepared for us. As soon as our headlights flashed on his building, Mathias was striding outside with a gurney in front of him.

"That man is *fine*. He's like Dr. Dreamy on that show."

"*Grey's Anatomy*?"

"Sure, whatever. Less talk. More looking," Miss Elva ordered.

I snapped my mouth shut. We watched as Mathias stopped to admire Luna behind the wheel of the cop car before pulling her out and dipping her in a decidedly long kiss. We both sighed.

"I bet they'll be doing some roleplaying later," Miss Elva said.

"I'm jealous."

"Now, Althea. You can't be jealous. You have options. You're just being difficult. Or too picky. I can't decide."

"Okay, I'm not actually jealous. I love Luna and I'm happy for her. I'm just jealous of the dirty sex she'll have later."

"Once again, might I remind you that you can have all the dirty sex you want?" Miss Elva gave me a look.

"I'd have to find a new candidate. The current ones come with complications."

"So? Find a new candidate then. Nobody likes a whiner, you know."

"Oh my goddess. I am *not* whining. I'm just pointing out that I would like dirty sex too."

"So? Go get some then."

"Who…what…dirty sex?" Chief Thomas croaked from the back of the Land Rover, and I whirled to see him sitting up and rubbing his hand over his face. Heat flashed through my face.

"I…nothing. Just nothing. Chief, it's Althea and Miss Elva. We've taken you to the doctor because you were attacked."

"Attacked?" Chief Thomas shook his head and turned when the back hatch of the Land Rover opened.

"Chief! You're awake," Luna exclaimed, and Mathias reached in to hold Chief Thomas's hands. I immediately banished all thoughts of dirty sex because he was my best friend's boyfriend. Not to mention an incredibly kind man who had no problem taking another man's hand to offer comfort.

"Sir, you've sustained an injury. If you don't mind, I'd like to examine you to make sure you don't need to go to the hospital," Mathias said, his tone confident.

Chief Thomas instantly responded, nodding once and

sliding from the back of the car. Mathias wrapped an arm around his waist before he tried to stand and, in one smooth movement, lifted him to the gurney. My eyes widened at his strength and my gaze flitted to Luna, who grinned at me as heat flooded my cheeks.

"It helps to be strong in his profession," Luna said.

"I bet," I agreed, and Miss Elva and I shared a look before we got out of the truck and walked to the gurney.

"Althea." Chief Thomas blinked up at me.

"Chief. We found you lying on the ground by your car. You're safe now. Mathias is going to take care of you. I promise we won't go anywhere until you're a little more coherent."

"But…that could take hours," Miss Elva hissed, and elbowed me in the side.

"Oof. Fine, you can go. I'm staying." I elbowed her back.

"Thank you…" Chief Thomas blinked up at me.

"Let's get him inside. I want to check the site of the injury and all his vitals. I suspect he may have a concussion," Mathias said, his tone brisk as he ordered us about.

We followed them into the clinic, and I turned to lock the doors behind us – just in case. I didn't want to be looking over my shoulder every second while Mathias conducted his examination.

"We'll wait out here," I said, not wanting to distract Mathias as he worked, and Miss Elva and I made ourselves comfortable in the waiting room while Luna stayed with Mathias.

"That's gotta be a pretty bad hit if he was out for that

long," Miss Elva mused. "We might be dealing with a pretty strong witch."

"Unless they used like a baseball bat or something," I said. I kept one in my house because I couldn't trust myself to fire a gun straight. I'd likely end up hitting Hank, and then I'd never be able to live with myself if that happened.

"Or like a tranquilizer? That could knock him out easily. I didn't see any blood," Miss Elva pointed out.

"Hmm, now that I think about it, I didn't either." I picked up a recent gossip magazine and paged through it. You'd think that having recently been a subject of ridicule in one of these magazines would have turned me off them, but I was hopelessly addicted.

"He's running some toxicology tests," Luna said as she joined us in the waiting area. "There seems to be no injury or wound, and Mathias found what he thinks is an entry spot for a needle on the chief's neck. But...he says the entry looks messy. Bigger than a typical needle hole."

"Poison dart." Miss Elva nodded sagely and I gaped at her.

"Like when you blow through a tube and hit someone with a dart?" I asked.

"Yup. Mighty handy if you don't want to get too close to someone."

I opened my mouth to ask when Miss Elva would have used that, but Luna waved my question away with a flutter of her fingers. "That actually makes sense. So, the chief is in and out of consciousness. The last thing he says he remembers is leaning against the hood of the car and watching the road. If it's true he was tranquilized, then I don't think he'll be able to offer much more help on adding any clues."

"This person is really bold," I said.

"Sho' is," Miss Elva agreed. "But also they gotta be strong on their aim. You can't just pick up dart-blowing like in a weekend or something. There's a fine skill to it. Not to mention getting the right drugs to knock someone out but not kill them."

"That's also a good point." Luna nodded.

"What about a tranquilizer gun? Don't they have those when they have to like subdue a large animal but not hurt it?" I asked.

"Hmm, I suppose that makes more sense than the dart-blowing. That's a lost art, in my opinion."

"I…I have never put much thought to it being an art at all," I admitted.

"It really is. You have to put so much time and consideration into your shot. You have to judge the wind, the weight of your enemy, if your enemy is moving…" Miss Elva shook her head, sending her sequins shimmering. "It's not for amateurs."

Now I was really curious what enemies Miss Elva had taken down with a poison dart, but at that moment Mathias came out of the examining room holding Chief Thomas's radio. "Ladies, it appears there is a…situation at Theodore's house."

"Is that right?" Miss Elva leaned back and smiled.

"Yes, from the scanner operator it seems he is reporting a dead body banging at his back door."

"Hmm, that's too bad, isn't it, Althea? Well, I'm ready

for bed," Miss Elva stood and stretched her arms over her head. "Who is with me?"

"Miss Elva," Luna said, tilting her head.

"What? I'm tired. We just rescued a police chief, which, let me tell you, is not typically in my job description. It's been a long day. Best to rest up so we can handle what comes tomorrow."

"Fine by me," I said cheerfully, and stood to gather my purse.

"No. That is not how we operate," Luna said, and crossed her arms over her chest.

"But…" Okay, maybe I did whine on occasion.

"You don't get to play favorites with who you help," Mathias said, shrugging a shoulder, "Listen, as a doctor, especially when I'm doing some of my ER rounds, I have to admit there's some people I might not want to help. Maybe it's a guy who just beat up his wife or something awful like that. But I can't pick and choose who I give help to, or then I become some almighty moral dictator of medicine. You ladies have the unique tools to address this situation."

"You're saying you want to send your girlfriend into harm's way?" Miss Elva glowered at Mathias.

"I'm saying that I trust Luna, I trust her power, and I trust her ethics," Mathias said, holding Miss Elva's eyes.

Surprisingly, she broke first. "I knew I shouldn't have gotten involved with you goody two-shoes." Miss Elva grumbled and stood, grabbing her handbag.

"I'm with you, Miss Elva. Theodore is a jerk."

"But we may get more clues," Luna pointed out, and

turned to kiss Mathias before joining us at the door. "Plus, it might give us more power over him."

"Hmmm…" I said.

"Oh please, we've helped that ninny before and he acts like nothing's happened two days later," Miss Elva groused.

"He has, hasn't he? When is he going to learn some humility?"

"Who knows? But maybe this time we'll teach it to him." Luna smiled and patted my arm before sliding in the passenger seat of the Land Rover. I busied myself with putting the back seats up and caught Miss Elva as she bent into the police cruiser and then danced her way back to the Land Rover.

"What did you just do?"

"Nothing, child. Nothing at all. Okay, let's go visit the fancy people of Tequila Key."

"I don't believe you," I said to Miss Elva, but was saved from conversation as she peeled away from the medical practice. I grabbed the handle and began to bargain with whatever goddesses were currently in charge of this little sitcom of my life.

"She's entirely too cheerful," Luna said over her shoulder to me, and Miss Elva flicked on her stereo to drown us out. In seconds, the car filled with the thumping beat of Beyoncé asking who ruled the world.

In this instance, it seemed Miss Elva did.

Chapter Eighteen

MISS ELVA SCREECHED the Land Rover to a stop in front of Theodore's imposing and boring – in my opinion – house in the hoity-toity section of Tequila Key. It was a neighborhood where houses were gated and often sat empty for part of the year while their owners summered in less humid climates. Stately pillars and a second story-wraparound porch dominated Theodore's white plantation-style mansion. It was from there he stood, shotgun in hand, and let loose a round toward the body weaving erratically across his yard.

"What the hell…" Miss Elva said, hopping from the driver's seat and stomping to the wrought-iron gate that ended in gold spikes at the top.

"He did not just unload a shotgun into a body in front of us, did he?" I asked Luna as we gingerly got out of the car.

"In all fairness, it looks like he unloaded it into his fancy topiary and not the actual body. It seems he needs to work on his aim."

"But it's a shotgun. Isn't that, like, dead easy to hit something with? I thought the bullets spread or something." My knowledge of guns was limited, but even I knew that shotguns were good for people who needed to command attention but had little prowess.

"Where did he go?" Luna wondered.

"The kick of the shotgun sent the damn fool ass over end on his porch." Miss Elva pointed to where Theodore's pajama-clad arm hooked the railing of his porch and heaved himself up, the gun waving wildly in the air. We all jumped behind Miss Elva's Land Rover. I was largely certain Theodore wouldn't shoot us, but I couldn't dismiss the fact that this might be the perfect time for him to rid the town of what he viewed to be vermin.

And I wasn't talking about the dead body weaving about his yard.

"Now you listen up, Theodore!" Miss Elva popped up and shouted, and then immediately ducked back down when the gun swung her way.

"Who is that? I can't see that far!" Theodore called out.

"Then maybe he shouldn't be pointing a gun our way?" I hissed to Luna.

"It's Miss Elva, Luna, and Althea. The chief has deputized us. And if you point that gun at me one more time, I'm going to have to take you in for threatening an officer of the law." Miss Elva used her "don't mess with me" voice and even I hunched my shoulders at her tone.

Officer of the law? I mouthed to Luna.

"She's put a badge on." Luna looked at me. "Did you give her a badge?"

"No, I most certainly did not." I sniffed. I wanted a badge.

"I'm being attacked!" Theodore shouted.

"Is anyone on the porch with you? Are you in immediate danger?"

"My wife is in the panic room. I'm defending our homestead," Theodore said.

"Panic room? He's got a panic room? I thought he'd be more the type for like a sex dungeon," I said.

"No way is he the sex dungeon type," Miss Elva said over her shoulder to me. "He lacks imagination."

"I suppose that's true. Panic room. Jeez." I shook my head. I could think of better things to spend my money on. Like a spa bathroom. Or an infinity pool. But, judging from the size of their house, they probably had all that. Maybe a game room? A ping-pong table would be fun.

"Why don't you just get yourself a ping-pong table then?" Luna asked me, and I realized I'd been speaking out loud.

"Um, because I need someone to play with me? Plus, Hank would chase the balls and chomp on them and then I'd be in a never-ending loop of buying more ping-pong balls."

"What about one of those…" Miss Elva made a motion with her hand that looked dangerously close to a man jerking off, and I raised both of my eyebrows at her.

"I need you to elaborate. With words."

"The shuffle things, you know?" Miss Elva turned back to the house.

"I think she is talking about a shuffleboard table," Luna said.

"Oh, right. Hmmm, I suppose that's a thought. Have you played one?"

"Only at a bar. It could be fun. But maybe we get Beau to get one for Lucky's? It's more fun with a drink."

"Yeah, but if it is at Lucky's, we will always be fighting with other people to get access to the board," Miss Elva said.

"I suppose that's true," Luna mused. "Let's find a bar that has one first and try it out before you purchase."

"Sweet. Road trip." Tequila Key had a limited number of bars, so we'd need to go to the next Key over to search it out.

"Did someone say road trip? I'll get the snacks," Miss Elva said.

"Excuse me? Are you going to do anything?" Theodore screamed from the balcony, and we snapped back to attention.

"I told you, Theodore. As an officer of the law, I have instructed you to put down your weapon. I see you still standing there with it laying on your shoulder all cool as if you didn't just send yourself ass over end on the porch. I bet you've never even shot that bad boy before, have you? It's not wise to have guns in your home if you don't learn how to use them," Miss Elva scolded.

"Okay, okay, okay. I'm putting the gun down. Just… deal with that, will you?" Theodore waved his hand at the body in his yard like we were the cleaners who had to put away the mess from a party.

"I don't like the way you're speaking to us right now. It sounds very condescending. Have you ever considered using manners? Maybe if you ask politely, we'll handle this for you." Miss Elva put her hands on her hips.

"Where is Chief Thomas?" Theodore yelled.

"He's incapacitated. We are working on his authority because we have the special and, might I say, highly expert skill set to deal with this particular problem of yours. However, I do have the discretion to pick and choose which cases I will handle. And my colleagues and I do not work with people who are rude or condescending."

"How have I been rude?" Theodore demanded.

"You pointed a shotgun at us."

"I don't have my contacts in. Everything's fuzzy," Theodore complained.

"We told you who we were. I literally just yelled at you that Miss Elva is here. And you had the nerve to point a gun in my direction? Where I grew up, that would get you killed on the spot. Just consider yourself lucky that I'm a refined woman now who has outgrown such impulsive instincts."

I heard a thwacking sound and craned my neck to see Miss Elva slapping a billy club into her hand.

"How did she get a billy club?" I asked Luna.

"I have no idea. Maybe that's what she took from the squad car?"

"I don't think she needs to be armed. Her magick is arsenal enough. Miss Elva with a billy club is…terrifying." A shiver ran through me at the thought.

"I've put the gun down," Theodore said.

"Hands up," Miss Elva ordered. Theodore put his hands up. "Now turn around."

"Why?"

"Do as I say!" Miss Elva barked, and Theodore turned around.

"Now twerk," Miss Elva ordered, and I rounded the hood of the Land Rover at that.

"I don't know how!" Theodore pleaded.

"You're abusing your power," I said to Miss Elva, tapping the badge on her chest, "Don't be like this."

"Oh, right. I swear, it can go to your head really quickly." Miss Elva glanced down at the gold star pinned to her chest.

"We're better than this."

"We're not, but Luna is." Miss Elva sighed and called out to Theodore, "Just stay turned around. We're going to make sure your house is secure and the only damage to your property is from the bushes you've been shooting at."

We went to the gate but were stuck when it refused to budge open.

"This gate is locked closed," Miss Elva called.

"My wife hit the panic button. Everything locks and the system overrides," Theodore called down. "You'll have to go over it."

We eyed the gold spikes at the top of the gate.

"Like hell… " Miss Elva said, and she and Luna bent their heads together. In moments, they'd pulled some items from their bag, cast a small circle of which I was not a part – and I won't lie that stung just a little bit – and began their spell. I stepped back to give them clear berth and gasped when the gates blasted open, popping from the hinges and one of the doors landing with a crash on the water fountain, where a large-breasted woman fed a fish.

"What was that?" Theodore screeched, but to his credit he kept his back turned.

"Oh, just standard police battering ram to open your gate."

"A battering ram! You just said there would be no more damage."

"That was before we knew that the gates couldn't be opened. This is for your own safety," Miss Elva called up as we hightailed it around the corner of the house where we'd last seen the body dance away.

"Isn't he less safe now that he has no gates to protect him?" I said to Miss Elva once were out of Theodore's sight.

"Child, how is a gate that doesn't open safe? If he needs to make a run for it...where is he going? In circles around the yard? I just gave him freedom."

I couldn't really argue with that.

"He's over here," Luna said. She pointed to a body sitting on a swinging chair bending his nose to a rose on a bush. It was a lovely spot, bathed in moonlight and surrounded by flowers. Too bad the smell of rotting flesh overpowered the scent of flowers.

"I know I need to leave." The corpse sighed and stood up.

"I'm really sorry about that," Miss Elva agreed. "We have some questions before you leave."

"I just wanted a moment of silence. I miss my gardens. It's what I used to do, when I was alive. I was a landscaper. Being in nature gave me such peace."

"We can give you a little time with your flowers if you'd like," Miss Elva said.

"We can?" I whispered to Luna, who elbowed me in the side.

"No, it's okay. I'll know you're here and it will take the enjoyment away."

"You don't like being around people?" Miss Elva asked.

"Very few people are worth being around. I do miss my family, though. It was nice, you know, to hear someone call me Daddy once again," The corpse shrugged a shoulder. "But you aren't my family. So I'll go."

"Wait…" Luna said, and then we all drew a collective breath in as the body crumpled to the ground and the soul hovered over it for a moment.

"You can stay just a little longer," I said, trying my best to smile sweetly at the man.

"I'd rather not." With that, the ghost disappeared and I turned at Rafe's laughter behind me.

"You can't even keep a ghost man around," Rafe hooted, doubled over in the air behind me.

"It wasn't just me!" I exclaimed. "He didn't want to be around any of us."

"I'm certain it was just you. It wasn't my lovemountain he was looking at when he vanished."

"He's really wearing on my nerves." I turned to Luna, who patted my arm gently.

"Don't let the haters get to you, Althea."

"Rise above, Althea. Take the high road," Miss Elva agreed.

"Oh? When have you ever taken the high road?" I asked.

"I always take the high road. I am the definition of the

high road. Look at this..." Miss Elva gestured to her sequins.

"You just tried to make Theodore twerk in his pajamas," I pointed out.

Miss Elva quickly changed the subject. "Are we going to clean up this body or not? Because if we leave it here, Theodore's going to blow up this whole neighborhood."

"That's what I thought..."

Chapter Nineteen

"OKAY, YOU LIFT THE BODY," Miss Elva said, studying her nails and then looking up at me.

"Me?" I asked, pointing at my chest. "Why don't you?"

"Because I just got my nails done. And I know you don't care about your nails."

"That is absolutely untrue," I protested as I curled my fingers into my palm to hide my chipped polish. Maybe I didn't get manicures weekly, but I tried to keep my finger-nails neat and clean.

"Then why are you hiding your nails?" Miss Elva asked.

"I'm not hiding them. I'm just clenching my fists in case I need to pop you one for not helping out," I said, jokingly lifting a fist. When Miss Elva raised her billy club, I shrank behind Luna.

"You're already dirty and smelly from the corpse earlier this evening," Miss Elva said.

"She has a point," Luna murmured to me.

"She's terrifying with a billy club. You have to take it away from her," I whispered to Luna.

"Miss Elva," Luna said, stepping forward and turning on her charm. "I think it's best if you let me hold that billy club for you."

"Why? It's not safe to go around these parts unarmed. Especially, you know, with people like him around." Miss Elva nodded toward the front of the house, where Theodore was likely having an apoplectic fit by now.

"While I'm sure that's true," Luna laid a soothing hand on Miss Elva's arm, "I don't think you're ever really unarmed, are you? Not with the wealth of power you have at your disposal."

"I guess you're right." Miss Elva sighed and looked down at her club.

"Plus it doesn't go with your outfit. I think you'd want more sequins for that look," Luna said.

"That's true. I wonder if they make sparkly clubs," Miss Elva said, and handed off the club to Luna, who immediately tucked it away in her bag.

"I could bedazzle one for you if you'd like," I offered, and then clamped my mouth shut. I really didn't need to offer Miss Elva more weapons.

"I'd like that for Christmas, please, if you're taking notes." Miss Elva put her nose in the air.

"Duly noted. Now, about this body? Because I'm going to be honest...I'm still not sure if my stomach is strong enough from my last encounter with a dead body. I don't think I can go any closer."

We all turned as a car door slammed and someone rounded the corner of the house.

"Ladies. I've been dispensed to assist with the…situation." Joseph Meden, the coroner and apparently also body-mover, crossed the garden.

"Who sent you?" I asked.

"Chief Thomas heard the call on his radio and said it was another situation like we'd had before. Is, um, everything clear here? I'm okay to do my work?" Joseph tugged on the ball cap he wore and decidedly did not meet any of our eyes.

"Yes, sir. You most certainly can go ahead. We were just discussing the best way to handle this." Luna dimpled at him.

"I've got it taken care of, ladies. So long as maybe you can handle the situation out front?"

"What's that?" Miss Elva demanded.

"Theodore is…" Joseph sighed and shook his head.

"Nothing more needs to be said." I nodded my thanks to Joseph, and turning we all trudged toward the front of the house, where strangled sounds greeted us from the front porch. Theodore sat on the front stoop in striped pajamas and struggled with his breath.

"Theodore, are you okay?" Luna, the nicest one of us, rushed to his side and kneeled in front of him.

"I don't know. I…I feel like this was a personal attack. On my property. On my liberty. On my freedoms!" Theodore gasped, pumping his fist in the air. His eyes glinted in the porch lights and looked glassy from shock.

"Um, hmmm. What exactly did you think you saw?" Luna slid a look to Miss Elva, and they did a silent communication thing back and forth. Miss Elva shook her head, and Luna nodded, and then Miss Elva stomped her foot. Finally, she seemed to agree to whatever Luna was demanding and walked over to ease herself down in front of Theodore.

"Why…a corpse, of course. The walking dead! A zombie. Sent to kill me. Sent to take over the world. They want to rule us, you know." Theodore nodded dramatically.

"Is that so? And what would be so bad about that?" Miss Elva asked.

"Why…they'd make us listen to rap music, of course," Theodore said, and we all stopped and looked at him like he was two crayons short of a box.

"You're saying that if the zombies become our over-lords, the worst thing you can think will happen is that we'll be forced to listen to rap music?" I asked, just to really clarify what I was hearing.

"The…*worst*," Theodore said, a haunted look on his face.

"You're not worried about the flesh-eating or all over general loss of control when a zombie virus rips through you? But the rap music? That's your limit?" Miss Elva asked.

"It's…unthinkable." Theodore shuddered.

"Can we just get rid of him?" Miss Elva turned to Luna. "Because we could just say the corpse got him."

"Joseph already saw him alive. We have witnesses." Luna smiled.

"We could…" Miss Elva began, and Luna raised a hand, her shoulders shaking in laughter.

"We are not taking out poor Joseph. The man is liter-ally doing our dirty work for us."

"Fine." Miss Elva turned back to Theodore and put her hands on either side of his face, forcing him to look in her eyes. "Theodore."

"Yes?"

"You didn't see what you thought you saw tonight."

"I didn't?"

"No. Remember, you don't have your contacts in. Well, you're going to feel really silly about this…but it was just a deer in your yard."

"A deer! Really? I was certain it was a body. My wife said she saw a body on the security cameras."

"I'll just go check on your wife." Luna disappeared inside, using her magick on the door to enter. I suspected she was going to breach the panic room and wipe the cameras, though I had no idea what magick she would be using for that particular feat.

"Oh, my wife! Is she okay? I love her, you know."

"We know you do." I said. Surprisingly, he really did love his wife. Though I was fairly certain he harbored a fascination with Miss Elva. But that was neither here nor there…

"Your wife is just fine. It was just a silly deer eating your bushes." Miss Elva held his face and muttered something under her breath.

"My bushes! I swear, no matter what I do those damn pests keep getting into my garden." Theodore seethed, and I could tell whatever magick Miss Elva was concocting was working.

"I understand. They really can be a nuisance. Luckily, we got the deer out for you, though you caused some damage when you shot at your gates."

"I…I shot at my gates? Oh, dear." Theodore shook his head sadly. "I just had those upgraded."

"You'll need to call your guy back to fix them," Miss Elva said, and glanced up as Luna slipped outside and gave us a nod. "It's best now you go get some rest. Everything's safe out here and you can go check on your wife."

"Right. I'll do that." Theodore stood and blinked down at us. For a moment I thought he was actually going to thank us for our help, but instead he turned and stomped inside, slamming the door behind him. We all heard the definitive *click* as the lock turned in the door.

"*Such* a nice man," I said.

"*Really* lovely," Miss Elva agreed.

We all turned as Joseph wandered around the side of the house, whistling, a black body bag slung over his shoulder. With a jaunty wave, he disappeared to his car.

"Well, I guess that's it. I mean…we only have to work in like…" I looked at my phone. "Four hours?"

"Can't you take the day off?" Miss Elva asked.

"I really try not to cancel on clients."

"Then I guess we'd better go," she said.

"Did we learn anything useful tonight? I mean, seriously. I'm covered in dead body bits, I smell like butt, and I'm out a good night's sleep," I said.

"Yeah, we did learn something. That somebody's got a daddy fetish," Miss Elva mused.

"Grosssss," I said.

"She's escalating," Luna said as we all stood and walked to the Land Rover, gingerly stepping around the broken gates.

"Two bodies in one night." Miss Elva opened her door and hauled herself in the front seat.

"And she's upping her game. Taking out the chief of police is serious business," Luna agreed.

"And with poison. So…yeah. All in all?" I asked.

"We've got a monster-sized problem on our hands."

Chapter Twenty

I WOULDN'T SAY that I was in the best mood when a knock woke me and Hank up the next morning fifteen minutes before my alarm was set to go off. Sure, I typically rose about an hour earlier than it currently was, but that was after nights when I had a regular evening of watching a Bravo show and sneaking a pint of ice cream in bed. On nights where I had to spend forty-five minutes showering at three in the morning to get the smell of dead people off me, I was entitled to sleep in until the last possible moment.

"I may become stabby," I told Hank as he raced from the bedroom and clattered down the stairs, skidding to a stop by the door while I was still tying my bathrobe around me. Hank's barking kicked up to a fit, and I paused when I heard a voice.

"Hey, buddy. Is your mama home? Her bike is still out front."

Trace. Damn it. He'd let himself in with his key. I hadn't even taken a moment to look in the mirror.

"Hey," I said, rubbing sleep from my eyes and waving vaguely in his direction as I plodded toward the coffeemaker. I didn't have much time before I had my first client of the day, so I needed to start mainlining caffeine as soon as possible.

"I brought coffee."

"Oh, I love you." I changed course and beelined for Trace, automatically throwing my arms around him in a hug like I would have done any other time. Except this time things were different, and I wasn't sure if that had been the right move.

Letting my arms drop, I pursed my lips and looked up at him.

"And I love you back. You look like you need this, though." Trace grinned at me and I felt some of the tension that still hovered around us ease.

Taking the cup of coffee he offered me, I slugged some down even though it burned my mouth and moved across the room to feed a dancing Hank.

"Rough night?" Trace asked, and I looked up to see him glance upstairs and then around the house. It suddenly dawned on me that he was still hovering near the door.

"Come on in. I've got just a little bit of time before work and I need to let Hank out." I realized that Trace wasn't sure if I had company. Though I was flattered that he thought I was capable of reeling men in left and right, who had the time when dead bodies were wandering the streets?

"Thanks. I brought breakfast sandwiches too."

"Oh, you are truly a savior."

After Hank gulped his food down as though I didn't

serve him two square meals a day plus treats, I pulled a fuzzy yellow tennis ball from his drawer and he almost convulsed in excitement. I could mirror the sentiment with the delicious scents coming from the food bag Trace carried past me to the couch on the back verandah.

"Go get it, buddy," I said. Launching the ball across the yard, I watched as Hank zipped across the grass. I wished I could bottle his energy sometimes.

"He's always so happy," Trace observed, handing me a sandwich, and I smiled my thanks as I unwrapped an egg and cheese biscuit.

"I know. I sometimes wish I could just live in his world. Simple needs, simple joys. He doesn't ask for much."

"Not feeling very joyful lately?" Trace looked over at me.

I paused, really looking at him now that the caffeine had begun to work its magic on my brain. He looked good. Lightly tanned as always, his blond hair in riots around his head, sunglasses hanging from his neck. He wore a long-sleeved rash guard with the logo of his company on it, and I knew it meant he had clients booked for dives today.

"Trace, I miss you," I admitted, and held his eyes. "I miss us. Whether we ever try dating again or we work as friends, I just miss the ease of what we had. I don't want to lose our friendship, and we promised we wouldn't. But now we're doing this weird kind of avoiding each other thing, and I don't know how to handle it."

Well, that was not what I was expecting to come out of my mouth, but I mentally patted myself on the back for being forthright.

"I miss us, too, Althea. And I agree. I don't know that we'll make it as a couple, at least not until you get over some of your commitment fears. And I really don't want to lose you in my life."

"I don't want to be weird around you," I said.

"So don't be."

"But what happens when I see you with a girl? It might have bothered me a little before, but I think it will bother me a lot now. And yes, I am well aware that makes me sound very hypocritical."

"So you want me to exist as your friend who suddenly is asexual?"

"Yeah, that will work for me. Cool for you?" I smiled, lightening my words.

"I think it will be weird for both of us to see each other with someone else. At least for a while. Or maybe until… you go to therapy."

"Excuse me?"

"Or…we. We can go to therapy," Trace quickly amended.

"Like couples therapy?"

"I don't know. I was just throwing it out there. I think we've got some good stuff going. But it also feels like you're always looking for an exit strategy. Even when I was staying here most days, it never really felt like my spot too. It was you letting me be in your space, but not us hanging out in our space together."

"Hmm," I said, leaning back to think on it. Frankly, it was the most Trace had ever really opened up about his insecurities in our relationship, and I didn't want to dismiss him. "I guess I also felt like you still had a lot of wanderlust in you."

"I do. But that doesn't mean we can't wander together, you know."

"Oh." I hadn't really thought of it like that.

"So now what?" Trace said, bending to pick up the ball and launch it across the yard for Hank. Hank always loved it when Trace came over as he could throw way farther than I could.

"I guess I do have commitment issues," I said.

"Duh," Trace laughed.

"And I don't know how quickly I can just…change that either," I said, finishing my coffee and putting the cup on the table while I gazed out to the water.

What Trace was asking of me sounded uncomfortable and a lot like…work. Emotional and messy work. Which were things that I typically avoided. However, sometimes you do things for the person you love that push you out of your comfort zone. This must be one of those things.

"I understand." Trace shrugged a shoulder.

"I'm not saying no. I think that you are likely right. I should talk to someone about this. But I don't think it will change overnight."

"So…you'll work on it and…what? I kind of hang out until you say come back?" Trace laughed and ran a hand through his curls.

"Yeah, that sounds really shitty, no?"

"It really does."

"I've decided not to date anyone for a while anyway. It's not like I'll be bringing anyone home. This is probably a good time for me to focus on some self-growth."

"That's fair. I'm not interested in dating right now either. I'd like to just get my head on straight," Trace said.

"So we aren't dating other people, but we aren't dating each other?" I sighed.

"I know. That also sounds like shit, doesn't it?" Trace laughed again. "We're ridiculous. How about this? No rules on the dating stuff, but let's just make one rule with each other."

"What's the rule?"

"Well, two rules. Let's not be weird, and let's always be truthful with the other. You're still my favorite person, Althea. I'd hate to think you were hiding things from me or had to tiptoe around me," Trace said, holding my gaze.

I lost myself for a moment, drinking in his pretty blue eyes. "I miss just texting you stupid stuff that happens during the day that I know you'll understand," I admitted.

"Then don't stop. Let's still be us."

"Okay, so no lies and no weirdness. And…" I took a deep breath. "I'll work on finding someone to talk to about…you know…my issues."

"Didn't you used to have a therapist?"

"Yes, but it's been a while. Maybe time to try someone new."

"Well, I'm open to it." Trace smiled and made a circle motion with his hand. "If it would be good for us, that is."

"Let me see what I can do with finding one I like first," I said, and scrubbed a hand over my face before checking the time on my phone. "I've got to run. We were up so late last night."

"Zombie stuff?" Trace pulled a sympathetic face.

"Major zombie stuff." I patted his shoulder as I passed

him, absolutely pleased that I didn't have to hide who I was or what I was about from Trace. I filled him in rapidly on my night while I brought Hank inside and packed my bag for the day.

"That's…wow. Two in one night? And his finger came off?" Trace grimaced.

"Right in my hand. I almost threw up."

"I'm worried about you. Can you promise me something? Just until this is cleared up?"

"Depends what it is," I said, and leaned a hip against the counter.

"Just stay in touch with me more, if you can. I know you've got Luna and Miss Elva, but sometimes you all three aren't together. It would help if I knew that you were safe. Maybe a panic word?"

"What's a panic word?"

"Like a word you can text me that lets me know you need help. I've still got your location shared on my phone."

"You do?" I'd forgotten we'd shared each other's location statuses on our iPhones when we were dating. At the time, it had made sense, but now it seemed like an oddly intimate thing to know of someone.

"Yes, do you want me to take it off?"

"No, probably for the best the way my life is going right now. Okay, a panic word." My eyes landed on Hank's stuffed cow that was peeking out of his toy drawer. "Moo."

"Moo? Like as in I'm a cow and I go moo?" Trace asked, a flash of grin lighting up his handsome face.

"Yes. Moo. If I moo at you, I'm in trouble. It's quick and easy to type."

"Fair enough. I'll keep an eye on my phone." Trace walked over and dropped a kiss on my cheek. "Take care of yourself."

"I will," I said, pleasure flowing through me at his kiss.

"Oh, I almost forgot." Trace turned at the door. "I have some clients coming in a few weeks or so. They want photographs of them underwater they can blow up for their living room."

"You can take those types of photographs." I rolled my eyes at Trace.

"I know. But they want artsy ones they said. Not just like 'hey, we were scuba diving on vacation.'"

"But…that's kind of what they'll look like underwater. Scuba divers. What with the gear and all," I pointed out.

"I think they want to try it free-diving. Something about an anniversary and a dress."

"Trace…" I groaned.

I really loved taking underwater photos. It was where I disappeared to in order to calm my brain. The pictures that came from those meditation sessions underwater were just a fun byproduct of something I enjoyed doing. I rarely took direct commissions, even more so if they were of people. I much preferred photographing fish over people. Fish didn't talk back.

"Just think about it. I'll email you details and you can be in contact with them if it's of interest to you. Plus, you haven't been diving in ages. Now that you've stopped avoiding me, you can come out on the boat again."

"I wasn't avoiding…" I sighed as he closed the door behind him, even though I could hear him laughing all the way to the street.

"Hank, you get to come to work with me today," I decided, knowing Luna was closing her side of the shop. "It's Bring Your Dog to Work Day."

Hank tilted his head at me as though to say every day should be bring your dog to work day.

"Fine, we'll discuss it with Luna," I promised him.

Chapter Twenty-One

I HADN'T HAD to send a "moo" text to Trace yet, and I was holding my breath that the streak would continue. It had been two days since he'd brought me a breakfast sandwich, and in that time I'd basically been waiting for the next call about a disturbance in the Force. Or, in this case, dead bodies terrorizing our little town. I wouldn't say that I was exactly relaxed, but after two days I did feel a bit calmer.

Chief Thomas had recovered successfully from his attack and it had been determined he was tranquilized with a fairly mild form of whatever it was they used to take down large wild animals. He was lucky he hadn't been attacked or harmed while he was out cold, and though I thought the experience had shaken him, he was grateful for our assistance at Theodore's house. From my understanding, Theodore was now going around town warning people of a large moose that was breaking down gates and terrorizing rose gardens, and most people were giving him the side-eye like he'd finally taken the jump off the deep end into Crazy Town.

"I told him it was a deer." Miss Elva shrugged as she clambered up my porch steps that morning. "That fool is going around warning people about a moose."

"You're certain you said deer?" I narrowed my eyes at her.

"You were there. What did you hear me say?"

"I heard you say deer. But I didn't hear your spell," I said, swinging the door wide and taking one of the bags she carried with her.

"Then I stand by what I said." Miss Elva stuck her nose up and hightailed it to my kitchen counter so she could put her other bag down and bend to pet a delighted Hank. He was torn between chasing Rafe and getting pets from Miss Elva. Cuddles won out, and once he'd lapped up his appropriate adoration from Miss Elva, he turned and raced after Rafe, chasing the horrified pirate ghost out into the backyard.

"That never gets old," Rosita commented from where she lounged on my couch.

"It really doesn't," I agreed.

Luna and Miss Elva were coming over this morning so they could set up for some big full moon spell they wanted to do in my garden that night. Apparently, I had the best outdoor space for whatever it was they were planning on doing. I hadn't even bothered to ask for details as it would all be explained to me when they were ready to tell me.

"I wonder why he doesn't chase you," Miss Elva said to Rosita.

"Because if a dog is running toward me, I will get

down and put my arms out and welcome the sweet furry beast into my cold, dead heart," Rosita said.

I had to agree with her – it was pretty much my standard response whenever I saw any dog. Especially if the dog decided it wanted to be my friend.

Dogs just made life that much sweeter.

"Whereas Rafe runs away from dogs. Hank just thinks it's a big game. He loves chasing after things. I think he sees Rafe as one big chew toy," I said.

"I heard that!" Rafe shouted as he streaked past the window, Hank on his heels.

"Do you squeak?" I called out to Rafe.

His answering shriek was all I heard. I looked to Rosita who lifted her hands as though to say, "close enough."

"Good morning," Luna said. She swept in the door looking as minty fresh as those people on the toothpaste ads who were up bright and early with the sun – fully coifed and anticipating a sunshiny day ahead of them. Luna was dressed in what for her was casual wear: a simple linen maxi skirt the color of stone and a loose silk white tank-top. An amethyst necklace hung at her chest, and diamonds sparkled at her ears. No dark circles dared to mark her eyes, I noticed, though I still carried mine from my sleepless night two nights ago.

"You look fresh," I said.

"Thanks. I had a nice workout this morning." Luna breezed past me. Miss Elva caught my eye over her shoulder.

"Practicing cops and robbers, were you?" Miss Elva mused, and Rosita and I burst out laughing.

"What? No, a yoga session."

"Did you assume the position?" I asked, and Luna looked at the ceiling, clearly counting to ten. Maybe if she actually did yoga when she'd said she was doing yoga, then she wouldn't need to count to ten to regain her calm.

"What are you trying to insinuate?" Luna asked, her tone prim.

"Just that we saw how that fine man of yours looked at you driving that police car and then he all casually picked up Chief Thomas like he weighed nothing. Oh, child." Miss Elva fanned her face. "Gets me worked up just thinking about it."

"Oh." Heat flushed across Luna's face, and we laughed again.

"You've picked a nice specimen," Rosita commented. "He looks like he'd have staying power in the bedroom."

"Oh…he does," Luna said faintly, and we lost her for a second as she drifted away, clearly reminiscing on her morning.

"Helloooo," I said, snapping my fingers under her face and then laughing when she jolted. "Let me get you a coffee."

"You'd have that look on your face too, Althea, if you had a man," Rafe said, poking his head in the door and then bouncing back out with a laugh. He was like one of those internet trolls, ready with a nasty comment at a moment's notice and then disappearing before I could get a retort in.

"Or you could go to that new sex shop." Miss Elva nodded.

"I don't want a man right now. I'm doing just fine," I said.

Silence greeted me, and I sighed, piling my curls in a knot on top of my head and tying them with a hair tie. "Fine. Tell me about the sex shop. Aren't they all the same?"

"No, this one is only for women."

"How can it be only for women? Toys can be played with by anybody," Luna said.

"I mean, it's like…meant to be a luxury shopping experience. You know what I mean? Like you don't feel skeezy going in and there's some old, grizzled guy leering at you over the counter and the last thing you want to do is put your purchase on the counter and envision his gnarled hands touching your new best friend." Miss Elva shuddered.

"Ew. That's why there's online shopping," I said.

"Sure, but this is cool because it's run by like young, hip, and fashionable people who know the products, you know? Like they can tell you if an oil is organic or what product is eco-friendly. It's all lit up real nice and luxurious, and you can even have a glass of champagne while you shop. It's like the Chanel of sex shops."

"Are you serious? I've never heard of this concept. It sounds way better than a place you stop in to buy an inflatable doll for a bachelorette party," I mused. Miss Elva was selling me on this. "What's it called?"

"Me Time."

"Not bad," I said. "It sounds like going to the spa."

"Except your massage will actually finish with a happy ending," Miss Elva said, and then wrinkled her nose. "That was a little low brow for me."

"I expect more of you," Luna agreed.

"Anywho…coffee, anyone?" I asked before the conversation completely derailed.

"Yes, perfect, thank you," Luna said, and put her own tote bag on the counter. Dutifully, she bent to pet Hank, who had come inside to press his nose against her leg. Hank had a particular soft spot for Luna, as she was my oldest friend and he'd known her ever since he'd become a part of my life.

"So you're still going to work today, right, Althea?" Miss Elva asked me. Today she was outfitted in a simple – for her – silver caftan and neon-green tennis shoes.

"Yes. I only have a half day like I usually schedule on Fridays, but one of my clients has waited months for this appointment and I would feel awful cancelling."

"That's fine. We need some time to discuss what we think will be best for our spells tonight. We've had some disagreements on which route we want to take, so we're going to the books." Miss Elva gestured to her tote bag. "It's gonna take a little time for us to dig through it all."

"I do think we are heading in the right direction, though," Luna said.

"I think so too. But we need to get this right…or…" Miss Elva looked at me and then back at Luna.

"What? What are you not telling me?"

"Nothing. She's just worried you won't get the magick right," Luna said smoothly. Too smoothly.

"Is that really the concern?"

"And, well, depending on the spell we use, if it goes haywire you might not enjoy the outcome. But don't worry…it's nothing we can't handle."

"I'm not liking the sound of this. What exactly do you mean about 'the outcome'?"

Miss Elva looked at the time on her phone. "Shoosh, child, would you look at the time? Shouldn't you be on your way to work? I think your first client will be here soon."

"I know you're trying to distract me, but I don't have time to argue," I hissed, grabbing my bag and heading to the door. "Keep an eye on Hank, please."

"I will guard him with my life," Luna promised.

I froze at the doorstep. "Just what are you doing that you need to guard him with your life?" I asked.

"No, I'm just saying he's like my baby too. I would do anything for him. You know that," Luna said.

"Right, okay, well…bye, I guess." I left the house with one last narrowed backward glance, not particularly enthused about going to work anymore. Luckily, I'd only be in for a few hours. They couldn't do that much damage in that time. Could they?

Chapter Twenty-Two

I BREEZED through my first morning readings and was pleased that all three of my clients walked outside with a lightness to their step. Ultimately, my goal wasn't to make people happy, or then I wouldn't be entirely objective in how I conducted my readings. I did my best to be tactful, honest, and help to provide direction for people.

However, sometimes with a tricky reading, a client wouldn't like the answers they were getting. It was my job to make them understand that I couldn't change what the cards or my psychic sense was telling me just because they didn't like what they were hearing. Ever hear the saying "don't ask questions that you don't want to hear the answers to"? It was kind of like that when dealing with certain clients. Sometimes their emotional responses were difficult for me to manage, and I often had to take some time with one of Luna's tonics and sage my office to clear out lingering energy.

Today, though, I had easy clients. All three were career-focused women who were needing some guidance on which direction to take. I always loved talking to women about their hopes and dreams, and fully supported any ambitions. It was important to never be rude or piss on someone's dreams – just because they might not be yours didn't mean they weren't worthy. I always thought that so long as a person had something that brought them joy or gave them hope, they should always pursue where that took them. It pleased me to see the flush of pleasure on my client's faces when the cards gave them answers that aligned with their own gut instincts. Maybe sometimes that was all a person needed to hear to take a chance on themselves.

Giving myself a little pat on the back, I poured some seltzer water and pulled out a new deck of cards to wait for my next client. This was a new client for me, one who had booked months in advance.

I looked up when the chimes on my door sounded and someone pushed inside. Oftentimes I had clients come through Luna's door because not only was her shop beautiful and a lovely first impression for clients, but many of them also ended up stopping to purchase something on their way out after a reading. Today, I'd kept her side locked and had opened the door in my space so clients could walk directly inside. However, because I kept my shop dim and moody – the mood befitting what clients expect when they go to a psychic – I was momentarily blinded whenever someone first pushed through the door to my office.

"Missy Sue!" I said, dropping my fake client smile and offering her a confused look. "Did we have an appointment today? I'm so sorry, I don't think I have it on my calendar. Let me look." I pulled my calendar from my tote bag. I liked to write all of my appointments down as well as schedule them online because I didn't trust computers – or I should say that I didn't trust my prowess with computers – and it was best to have a back-up paper copy.

"Oh, no, I'm taking over Marisa's appointment for her." Missy Sue beamed at me, "I was the one who recommended you to her. She called me this morning, dreadfully sick, and said she couldn't make it."

"That's too bad. She could have just called me and canceled it. We just had an appointment last week, though. Is there something else you really needed to talk about?"

"Oh, there absolutely is. You know how much I love my appointments with you," Missy Sue said, dropping into my guest chair and plopping her big Louis Vuitton bag on her lap. "That's not a problem, is it? For me to take the appointment?"

"Uh, no, it shouldn't be," I said, studying Missy Sue. She looked…off…today. Her eyeliner was smudged and she'd forgotten to conceal the dark circles under her eyes. And…her nail polish was chipped. I zeroed in on the polish, for some reason fixated on the crack in her veneer. It was just so unlike her to present herself like this. A warning sounded in my head.

"What's wrong?" Missy Sue said, and looked down at her nails. "Oh god, I know. I couldn't get into my same nail place. They're, like, all booked up this week. Which is crazy, because I spend a ton of money with them. But I don't trust the ones on the other end of town. By the new sex shop? I don't think they clean their tools. Stephanie got a toe fungus from going there."

"Ew," I said automatically.

"Right?" Missy Sue trilled, her laugh shrill and putting my back up a bit. There was definitely something wrong here. I wondered if she was planning to leave her husband or something. *So much for an easy day of readings*, I thought.

"I'll just get you a fresh pack of cards so the energy is all clear and we'll get started," I said, even though I'd just changed the pack of cards out. My instincts were sending me alarm bells, and I thought I'd better be smart for once. Bending over to grab a pack from my bottom shelf, I quietly slid my phone from my purse and opened my text application to type a message.

MOO.

"Did you hear there's a moose in town? Isn't that strange?" Missy Sue said as I popped back up and slid over the standard Rider Waite Smith tarot deck.

"I did hear that. I can't really wrap my head around there being a moose running around town. Don't they belong in the mountains?" I asked as Missy Sue shuffled. She was familiar with the routine and I let her go through the motions, my mind racing as I wondered if I was alerting Trace for no reason.

"I think so. Or are they in Vermont?"

"There's a mountain range in Vermont."

"Is there? Huh, who knew?" Missy Sue blinked at me and I painted a smile on my face.

"Yes, who knew?" Only, you know, most people with some geographic sense, I thought, but decided to leave that tidbit out. It was always best not to insult the intelligence of a client. Especially one who was looking a little bit stressed.

"Are you making fun of me? I'm not a cold weather person, so I don't really pay attention to the mountains. Though I do like the cute ski outfits." Missy Sue pursed her lips as she considered.

"No, I'm not. I don't think they are as big a mountain range as some others we have. I'm sure it's easy to over-look them," I quickly assured her, watching as she continued to shuffle while staring off into the air.

Back and forth she shuffled until I wanted to tell her that was more than enough, but thought better of it. Instead I waited quietly for Missy Sue to stop staring off into space and to refocus her eyes on me.

When she did, I kind of wished she hadn't. A flash of anger crossed her blue eyes before being replaced by the guileless look I had come to expect from her.

"What kind of reading can you do?" Missy Sue asked, finally laying the cards down. She didn't split them into three piles like she usually did, and so I waited, unaccount-ably tense, and watched her.

"What do you mean? Like what type of spread?"

"Sure. Like that. Say if I wanted to know a singular answer to something?"

"Well, you can always draw one card and look for a yes or no answer. Or we can do the one we often do, which is a Celtic Cross spread. As you will remember, that will still give you an answer to a question you're seeking, but sometimes provide deeper explanations and guidance to what you seek."

"What about like…foretelling the future?" Missy Sue

asked, nodding at my crystal ball. I didn't need the crystal ball to do those types of readings, but clients loved it.

"I can also do a psychic reading for you, but I often include that with the interpretation of the cards as well. Is that what you'd like?"

"What about talking to the dead?" The tone of Missy Sue's voice sent a chill across the back of my neck.

"Are you requesting a mediumship appointment? Those take much longer and cost more. Were you aware of the difference in pricing?"

"Why do they cost more?" Missy Sue's bottom lip poked out.

"Because more time and effort are involved. It's not particularly easy encouraging a spirit to revisit with a loved one, and it often depends on how far they've advanced into the spirit world. If so, it can take some time to get their attention and call them back. Working as a channel like that requires time and patience. And, I'm so sorry, Missy Sue, but I don't have time for that today if that is what you are looking for."

"But you're saying you could do that if you wanted to?"

"Of course, at the appropriately scheduled time," I said, watching her carefully.

"But what about the other day? When a book fell off the shelf? There was a ghost here, wasn't there?"

"Yes, there was." I saw no use in lying to Missy Sue. She was a dog with a bone, and until she got the answers she wanted, there was no way she'd drop this line of questioning.

"How come that ghost can just hang around but

others…won't visit you?" Missy Sue's voice hitched, and for a moment I thought she might cry.

"It's…well, it's different, Missy Sue. For each spirit, it's a different journey. I can't really speak for all ghosts or apparitions. Some get tied here with unfinished business. Some need more time to accept that they are dead and aren't ready to transition through the veil. Others just like being here and seek out those who can see them and can interact with them."

"So that one who was here the other day, they sought you out?"

"Um, something like that."

"Explain," Missy Sue barked, and I jumped.

"Missy Sue. Is this how you want to use your appointment time?" I nodded toward her cards. "Remember, if we talk the whole time, you won't get much time with the tarot cards."

"Answer. The. Question."

"The one who was here the other day didn't seek me out. I accidently pulled her through when I was working… on something else." I couldn't bring myself to explain magickal spells to her, or we'd be here all day.

"It was a spell, wasn't it? You brought this ghost over and now they are just hanging out here like every day?" Missy Sue's voice rose.

"Yes, well, something like that. The ghost can go where she wants. But she often chooses to hang around people who can see and hear her."

"So you know how to bring people over and have them stay."

"Not really." I pinched my nose. "It was more of an accident when I was working with Luna."

"Luna knows how. Of course," Missy Sue said, nodding. "She's really got her act together."

"I...um..." I wasn't sure how to interpret that. On one hand, she was directly insulting me, but on the other hand she was also correct in that Luna did, indeed, have her act together.

"She's not here today."

"Luna? No, she's at my house," I said automatically. And then almost kicked myself for telling her where Luna was.

"Why?"

"She's watching Hank for me."

"Why not just bring your dog here?" Missy Sue asked.

"Because sometimes he can distract clients. And I was supposed to have a new client today, so I didn't know how they would react to dogs. Missy Sue! Seriously! Let's stay focused. What can I help you with today?" I all but ground my teeth together and looked down at where my hands were clenched in my lap.

"I want to talk to my daddy."

When my eyes darted up in shock, a gun was pointed directly at my forehead.

Chapter Twenty-Three

"MISSY SUE," I breathed, not moving an inch. "What are you doing?"

"You are going to help me speak to my daddy," Missy Sue said, her blue eyes like ice as she stared me down. Her grip on the gun was rock steady, and I quickly reevaluated any impressions I had of Missy Sue only being a fashionista.

"It's you…" My hands clenched in my lap, but I made no moves. What could I do? I had a gun inches from my forehead. "You're the one who has been bringing back the dead bodies. How did you…where did you learn this stuff? You seemed so unknowledgeable about all things magick."

"Oh, please." Missy Sue stood and moved to the door, the gun never wavering from my head, and she flipped the lock. Her tone had lost some of its breathy and airy quality, and she sounded more jaded and sarcastic. Kind of like me, I thought. "Like magick is that hard to do."

"If it wasn't, why are you standing here pointing a gun at my head?"

Not smart, Althea, I silently berated myself.

"Is that how you want to play this? Insulting me? I have no problem putting a bullet in your head and stealing all your magickal shit. It's not like anyone will be all that surprised. You've got a reputation for hanging with the wrong crowd."

"Hey! I like my crowd," I protested.

"And lord knows what that yummy Cash ever saw in you." Missy Sue raked her eyes over me. "Would it kill you to use a little makeup? I mean, at the very least go to Sephora or something and get a consultation done."

"I wear makeup! Just not today because it's a half-day of work for me."

"A real woman puts her best face forward no matter what."

"I can assure you, I am certainly a real woman."

"It's no wonder you can't keep a man."

"I don't want a man!" I shouted, and Missy Sue actually laughed at me.

Was that the truth? Did I really not want a man? Maybe part of all this back and forth I'd been doing had everything to do with the fact that I just wasn't in a good space to have a relationship. There were so many crazy things happening in my life, from learning new magick to…well, this situation, that I guess I hadn't really given myself any time to process it all.

"Everyone wants a man, honey. Either to ride one or to drain one's bank account."

"I make my own money, Missy Sue."

"Then you still need one to ride."

"Not always. There's toys. Have you been to the new

sex shop? I heard it's like the Chanel of sex shops." *Keep her talking*, I thought, as my hand inched slowly toward the crystal ball on my table.

"Is it really? That might actually be fun. Not that it can replace the real thing, but it's good for a woman to have options in her toy chest. If you move your hand one more inch, Althea Rose, I will blow your ear off."

"My ear!" I said, aghast, as fear flickered through me. "Why my ear?"

"Because it's not enough to kill you, but you'll stop talking and take me seriously."

"Trust me, I am taking you very seriously right now. Missy Sue, do you even know how to shoot that thing?"

"Of course I do. My daddy was an expert marksman. I learned before I could ride a bike."

"For real?" I was trying to imagine a toddler with a gun.

"Sure. Watch, I'll take off your skeleton's pinky nail." Before I could shout at her to not hurt Herman, she pulled the trigger.

I gaped as the sound of the gun reverberated around my office, causing my ears to ring and tears to fill my eyes. Turning, I saw Herman's arm dipping to the side and the last bit of his pinky finger gone. She'd also shot a lovely hole in my back wall, but I didn't have time to wonder what the rest of the damage was before she rounded the table.

"Now, we're going to go to your house and get Luna and you will both help me speak to my daddy."

Her words sounded fuzzy, and I blinked at her for a moment. "My ears are ringing."

"Oh, right. Sorry about that. I have these little earbuds, see?" Missy Sue turned her head just enough that I could see little flesh-colored buds in her ear.

"Lovely," I said, pitching my words likely louder than they probably needed to be.

"So. Let's go."

"Wait. Hold on. Just…let me get my hearing back." I needed a moment to process everything. Plus, I felt like being able to hear would be a vitally important survival skill over the next few minutes, hours…whatever this would take.

Missy Sue sat back down with the gun trained on me. She wasn't good at waiting; I noticed her foot tapping the pole. Out of boredom, she slipped a card from the tarot deck and flipped it over.

The Tower.

I closed my eyes in gratitude. I knew what the cards were telling me.

"The ringing is going down. Let's just give this a moment, though, okay?"

"Fine, I've got all day." Missy Sue shrugged.

"Listen…why don't you tell me about your father? Maybe if I can get an idea of why it's so important you speak to him then I'll better be able to channel him when the time comes. Also, why didn't you just go this route to begin with?

"Holding you at gunpoint?" Missy Sue raised a perfectly groomed eyebrow at me.

"No. Using a medium."

"I tried, but you said he couldn't be contacted with tarot."

"No, not with tarot. But there's other ways. I even advertise those services."

"I need information. Sensitive information. I just wanted to talk to him alone." Missy Sue sighed.

"You miss him."

"Of course I miss him. I was his princess."

"I'm so sorry you've lost him. I can imagine the pain is terrible."

"Oh please, it's not just the pain. It was the fact that he gave me everything I ever wanted. You think my shitbag husband does that for me? No! He's always talking about budgets and…" Missy Sue wrinkled her nose. "Buying things at outlet stores. Do I look like the type to shop outlet stores?"

"No. But honestly, you can get some pretty killer deals," I said.

"Yes, I'm not surprised you shop there." Missy Sue gave me a pointed look.

"Missy Sue! I am *not* poor. I make good money for myself. But why pay one thousand dollars for a purse if you can find the same purse for four hundred dollars? It just makes sense!" Was I really arguing being fiscally responsible with a woman who wanted me to contact her dead father at gunpoint?

"If you like last season's purses." Missy Sue sniffed, and I guess that meant the subject was closed. Wasn't the point of buying a nice bag so that it would be timeless and you could wear it for years? I swear I'd read somewhere that Chanel bags held their value for ages.

"Tell me about the necromancy. It's…an odd and very

difficult choice for what you're trying to achieve. How did this even come to you?"

"You think you're the first psychic I've gone to? I've been up and down the state talking to psychics, voodoo ladies, healers, mediums…and nothing. Nobody has given me anything to go on. Except for this one man…I found him in the Everglades. A swamp man. Like a shaman. I think."

I'd seen some of the swamp guides in the Everglades and had a good idea of just what kind of person she'd stumbled upon. "Hmm. Go on."

"And he gave me a book. I spent a week with him and drained him of his secrets."

I made a mental note to talk to Chief Thomas about looking for the body of a lost swamp guide.

"He was the first one I brought back," Missy Sue said, pursing her lips as she thought about it. "It really wasn't pretty. But, man, what a rush, you know? Like I get it now. I get why you guys do this. So much power! It's a trip, isn't it?"

"Um, I don't know about that…I think it's really nice to help people."

"Sure, help people." Missy Sue tossed her blonde hair. "It's about the power and you know it. You hold people's fate in your hands. You can direct them on any path you want. I mean, how cool is that?"

"There's a responsibility in this profession, Missy Sue. You don't try to control what people do. You try to help them. And I need to be very clear here – I hold no one's fate in my hands but my own. We all decide our own paths."

"Be that as it may, my path is saying it's time for you to stop talking and for us to get our butts to your house."

"All so you can talk to Daddy?" I pitched my voice a little high to mimic her and then shivered when she glared at me.

"It's not just to talk to him, you idiot. I need to know where the key is."

"What key?"

"To his safe deposit box. I know he's left his fortune there. And then I can finally hightail it from this shitty little town and go live the life I'm meant to live."

"But why can't you do that now?"

"Because I need money. God, you're dumb."

"But just take some money from your husband and go then."

"He won't give me the account numbers." Missy Sue pouted. "And the bank refused to let me have them even though I showed proof of marriage."

"You could get a job," I said, and rocked back when Missy Sue banged the gun on the table.

"Women like me don't have to work. We either give good blow jobs or we inherit money. Understood?"

"Um, sure, I guess. Let me just get my purse. It's on the shelf down here."

"Leave it."

"I need it for my house keys."

"But Luna is there."

"And if she left for lunch?"

"Ugh, fine, stop whining. Grab your purse and walk slowly in front of me."

"Of course." I gave zero shits about my keys, but I did

care that my iPhone was tucked in my purse and my location had been shared with Trace. Now all I could do was hope that he wasn't on a dive and was able to get the help needed.

Or I was going to be dead meat.

Moo, indeed.

Chapter Twenty-Four

SHE MADE me drive her car home, and I tried to go as slow as I could until she pressed the gun to my rib cage.

"We're five minutes from your house. I honestly don't care if I shoot you now and I just go take Luna hostage. Either way, one of you bitches will get me the information I need."

"Okay, okay," I said, squirming in the seat, "Why did you keep going with the bodies if it wasn't working? Like, wasn't that gross?"

"Kind of. But I have a strong stomach for these things. I used to hunt and skin the animals after."

Really, my impression of Missy Sue had taken a ninety-degree turn.

"Huh. Okay then. So, I mean, were you able to communicate with any of them? They talked to me," I said.

"Did they? Damn it. I knew I should have stayed around longer. Mostly, I couldn't understand them because they didn't have tongues. They weren't my daddy, right?"

I really needed her to stop referring to her father as "daddy" but decided this wasn't the time to press that point home. "Not that I'm aware of. I can see ghosts, though, Missy Sue. Not everyone has that ability. It's not even really something you can learn from a book."

"I know. I tried. It's infuriating, but I had to accept my limits."

She did not strike me as a woman who knew how to accept her limits.

Pulling in front of my house, I closed my eyes for a moment when Hank's little ears popped up at the windowsill. "Here's the deal, Missy Sue. I promise you that I will get you the information you want. Even if it takes me weeks or whatever we have to do. Even if you get caught, go to jail, and still don't have the information – I will hunt your father's spirit down and get you the information you seek. But only on one condition."

"Okaaay." Missy Sue drew that out.

"You do not hurt my dog."

"As if! What kind of monster do you think I am?" Missy Sue gaped at me, and I was surprised to feel genuine waves of hurt coming from her. "Jesus, Althea. That's cold. I'm actually insulted you would think that of me."

"I…hmm." The crazy was strong with this one. "Then we have a deal."

"I noticed you didn't mention Luna, though."

"I don't think you'd hurt her. She's exceptionally helpful, particularly in this area."

"That's fair. It would be stupid to destroy an asset. Okay, let's go, sugar. It's time to have a little chat with my daddy."

I considered my options for a moment as I went to leave the car. I could roll out and try to run away, but I wasn't all that coordinated. I could honk the horn like crazy, but that would likely get me shot. Nothing I could think of was going to provide any reasonably good outcome.

"Althea?" Luna called from the front door, and my decision was made for me.

"Let's go," Missy Sue said, hiding her gun behind her handbag and pushing me in front of her.

I smiled brightly as Luna stood in the doorway. Hank whimpered and stepped back, causing Luna to glance down at him in worry.

"Gosh, you look tired. Rough morning?" I said. Which was something I never, ever said to Luna because, well, she always looked amazing.

Her eyebrows shot up as she looked between me and Hank. "Missy Sue is here," she called to Miss Elva. "She's taking Althea for a makeover."

"Who else is here?" Missy Sue hissed, pulling her gun out and aiming it at my head as she shoved me inside.

"Just me, darling. Gosh, I haven't seen you in ages, Missy Sue. How's that dull husband of yours?" Miss Elva said from where she leaned casually against the counter, her hand tucked in a pocket of her caftan.

"Getting duller by the day. Which is why I'm on the way out."

"I see that. Not sure this is the way out I'd recommend, if I'm being honest with you, Missy Sue. I'm thinking you'd want a handsome man and a nice villa somewhere instead of jail, right?"

"Only fools go to jail," Missy Sue said, ushering us forward until we all stood by the breakfast counter and waited.

Hank ran to my side, and I looked at Missy Sue and then down to where Hank growled. "Missy Sue, I think Hank is worried for me. I don't want him to lunge at you and then scare us all. Can I just get him to a safe place? Where he won't distract us? We'll need him tucked away anyway if we are to do the spell."

"Go on. That door, right there." Missy Sue pointed to my powder room door, and I quickly bent to pick Hank up. Kissing his head, I tucked him in the bathroom and promised him tons of treats later. I hated to lock him away, knowing he would be scared for me, but it was the safest thing I could do right now.

"Missy Sue would like to speak to her father. She'll need us to do that. I've explained we might have the tools that would allow her to have a conversation with him."

"I think I've actually pulled his spirit pretty close," Missy Sue boasted. "I just haven't been able to get him into a body yet."

"That's a real shame." Miss Elva nodded. "Necromancy is a fine art, though. It takes years to perfect it. I can't imagine you've been practicing it for a while as your father didn't pass all that long ago, if I recall?"

"No, he hasn't. But I think I'm doing pretty good for where I'm at so far. I'm just tired of it all, though. I want to move on with my life. So, speaking of such, can we get on with this?"

"Um, which spell would you suggest for this, Luna?

Miss Elva? It appears she doesn't want me to act as a medium because she wants alone time with her father."

"Daddy and I need to have a little one-on-one. Particularly because the lawyers are claiming his money is with his newest wife."

Ah, it was really all starting to make sense now. I vaguely recalled her father's newest wife – a blonde like Missy Sue but a few years younger than her, if I remembered correctly. I had to imagine that had stung a bit.

"Okay, we can bring him to you, Missy Sue. Let's go out back and get the circle set up." Miss Elva made an after-you gesture and we all turned to step outside.

A light popped behind me, and I whirled in time to see a flash of silver and then Miss Elva had her knee pressed to Missy Sue's back, cuffing her wrists while Missy Sue howled. My mouth dropped open as Hank let out a cacophony of barking from the bathroom.

"What just happened? How did you do that?" I gaped.

"I knew I'd worn trainers today for a reason," Miss Elva said, standing up and looking down at her neon-green shoes. "I just felt like I'd need to move fast."

Fast and *Miss Elva* were not words I used together often unless we were talking about her prowess with men.

"I'm shocked. Where did you get the cuffs?" I stomped my foot on Missy Sue's back when she tried to turn. "They look to be police issue."

"Huh, that's odd. Me Time really sells the nice stuff, hey?" Miss Elva looked away.

I highly doubted the sex shop would sell cuffs of this caliber, but let it drop. Missy Sue jerked under my foot.

"Listen, ladies, I made a promise. We still have to do the spell so Missy Sue can talk to her father."

"What? You've got to be kidding me, Althea. It's dangerous to work that kind of magick under pressure or for ill intent," Luna admonished me.

"I get it. Trust me, it's the last thing I want to do. But I promised Missy Sue that I would do this if she didn't shoot Hank."

"A promise is a promise." Miss Elva nodded.

"And maybe it will stop her from trying this nonsense again if she gets out of jail. *If* she gets out…" I said loudly down to where she groaned at my feet and banged her forehead against the floor.

"She said his spirit is close. We could just do an entrapment spell?" Luna asked Miss Elva.

I hauled Missy Sue up and walked her out the back door. Once there, I looked around until I saw Hank's leash. I nodded at it, and Luna stopped talking long enough to hand me the leash. After moving over to the electrical pole at the corner of the backyard, I lashed a squirming Missy Sue to the pole and then did the one thing I'd been wanting to do since she shot my skeleton: I slapped her across the face.

"What the hell!" Missy Sue screeched.

"Yes! I love this kind of stuff. For once, Althea, you're really sexy to me right now," Rafe said over my shoulder.

"Shut it, Rafe."

"Who's Rafe?" Missy Sue looked around.

"One of our ghosts."

"Is Daddy here?" Missy Sue sobered instantly.

"Oh...daddy fantasies. Interesting..." Rafe whispered at my ear. "Keep going. Let's see how this plays out."

"Rafe, get out of my face," I ordered.

"I'm liking this new dominatrix side of you, Althea," Rafe said, but then flitted away when I turned on him.

"Such a pest," I mumbled.

"Who else is here?"

"Your father is not here yet. I'll tell you when he is. I'll do my best to make sure you can talk to him, but it may have to come through one of us."

"I want to speak to him on my own."

"You're not exactly in the position to make demands," I said, enjoying how the red marks of my hand had risen across her face.

"I just..."

"Take it or leave it."

"Take it." Missy Sue sighed.

"Fine. I'll be back. Don't go anywhere," I said, and then laughed at my little joke when Missy Sue glared at me. I went back to where Miss Elva huddled with Luna.

"Are we really doing this or was that you acting?" Miss Elva said, and then surprised me when she gave me a big hug.

I leaned into her for a moment, appreciating her warmth and sighed when Luna's arms came around me too. "We're really doing it. But thank you for helping me."

"Of course. Goddess knows I knew something was up when Luna said you were going for a makeover with Missy Sue," Miss Elva snorted.

"Because I don't need a makeover. Right?" I said, and both Luna and Miss Elva looked away. "*Right?*"

"Let's stay focused here. Luna thinks we need to just cast a net for all the spirits nearby. It sounds like she's probably brought dear ol' Daddy close, but for some reason he's avoiding her."

"She said she wants to know where his safe deposit key is. And that he owes her."

"Well, the dead do like to keep their secrets. We're going to have to force him to talk to her."

"How do we do that?"

"We'll do an entrapment spell. But be warned…there could be more bodies."

"Whyyyyyy." Okay, I definitely whined sometimes.

"Because some of the spirits will choose that as their option to speak with us. Let's just hope not too many," Luna said.

"What do you mean, let's hope not too many?" I repeated.

"We can't know how many are in the area."

"Yeah, like this could be like a zombie army," Miss Elva supplied helpfully.

"Not zombies," Luna sighed.

"Potato, pah-tah-to," I said.

"All right, let's get moving. We can't keep Hank in the bathroom too much longer. Poor boy will have a fit."

"Ready to meet Daddy?" I said, and stepped into the circle they'd created.

"I bet he's a real gem." Miss Elva winked at me.

Chapter Twenty-Five

"DO you need me for this spell or should I just...look after this hot mess in the corner?" I nodded to where Missy Sue was stomping her foot into my newly planted bushes. I sighed. Every time I tried to be domestic and add something fresh to the yard, I either killed it or something else did. My tomato plants had only just finally gifted me with one little tomato, and that was after six months of dedicated work at trying to keep them alive.

"We're good, Althea. You just go get Missy Sue to calm down. The neighbors are looking." Miss Elva nodded.

I sighed again. There wasn't much I could do about my reputation on this street anymore, but it would be nice if a few weeks of quiet could go by for my neighbors. I heard a back door slam nearby and cringed at the noise Missy Sue was making.

Striding across the lawn, I stopped in front of her and raised my hand again.

She spit at me.

Leaping to the side, I glared at her. Whatever look she saw on my face was enough to stop her trying that little move again, because I was not in the mood. I'd already filled my quotient of being around gross bodily fluids for…well, forever, if I had my say in it.

"*That* was rude."

"Eat shit," Missy Sue said.

"That's also rude. Have you no manners? Really, Missy Sue. I don't have to have my friends help you. There is nothing requiring that I keep my word to you. You've lied and killed your way to this point – what's to say that I can't do the same back to you? An eye for an eye? Except, of course, the killing thing, as that really isn't to my taste."

"How do I know your friends aren't just doing some stupid spell to pretend they know what they are doing? I've run into a lot of fakes out there."

"Because when your daddy arrives and tells you how disappointed he is in you, you'll know." I laughed when her face twisted in a snarl.

"I'm his princess. He'll be proud of how hard I've been trying to see him again."

"You know something? I may not always be the most street smart, but I have learned you can't argue with crazy."

Missy Sue hissed and opened her mouth to say something else, but then her face went slack with surprise as she looked over my shoulder. Whirling, I looked across my garden to the water's edge.

"I swear I just saw a head pop up from the water," Missy Sue said.

"No way."

We watched as the ripples marred the surface, and my stomach twisted. From years of scuba diving, I knew what it looked like when something was about to break the surface of the water, and I suspected I wasn't going to like what I was about to see. In seconds, a corpse popped from the water and rolled itself on my beach, scrambling for purchase in the wet sand.

"Ewwww," I breathed.

"Swimming zombies," Missy Sue whispered.

"I'm going to have nightmares about this."

We watched as the bodies began to pour in, the water kicking up in splashes as corpses arrived from the sea. I did my best to not have an actual full-on breakdown as the bodies began to wander my yard.

"Hey!" I shouted as one veered toward my tomato plants. "Don't you dare…aww, damn it! I just got my first tomato from that." It actually physically pained me to see the body stomping cheerfully on six months of my lackluster dedication to gardening. I couldn't say gardening was my passion, but hey – I'd tried, okay?

"What is she doing?" Missy Sue asked, and I turned to see Miss Elva gliding through the garden, like a silver angel of doom, tapping corpses on the head. After she tapped each one, the body would fall and a spirit would flit away.

"I think she's letting the spirits that aren't your father go."

"Is he here?" Missy Sue asked.

"I don't know." I turned to look at her. "It's hard to see

what spirit is here once it is in a body. You'll only know if they speak to you."

"Missy Sue?"

"And that, I believe, would be your daddy," I said as Missy Sue convulsed in tears. Turning, I saw a young body walk up to us – twenty years old at the most. My heart hurt for the family who had lost this young man, for he was far too young to have died.

"Daddy," Missy Sue cried, her blue eyes hopeful and swimming with tears.

"Missy Sue." The corpse stopped in front of us and shook his head sadly as he looked at his daughter.

"Sir." I nodded, feeling weird speaking to him as though he was my elder.

"The name is Nathan. And it seems you have my very difficult daughter tied up…I'm assuming for good reason?"

"Um, I believe it to be a good reason, yes," I said.

"Is it because she's been trying to pull me back? I've been doing my best to avoid her, but she finally got me this time," Nathan said.

"Daddy, no," Missy Sue whimpered.

"Well, it was really Luna and Miss Elva who were able to successfully bring you…" I let my words trail off and took a step back from both of them. It was probably not the best to argue semantics at this point.

"I just wanted to talk to you again. I miss you," Missy Sue said.

"I highly doubt that." Nathan shook his head. "What kind of trouble did you get into now?"

"I was just trying to bring you home. I hate that you left me. I'm your princess."

"Missy Sue, you know I call everyone princess. I'm horrible with names."

Ouch, I thought, and turned so I didn't have to see the hurt lash Missy Sue's face.

"*No*. I'm your princess. And you promised me you would always take care of me!"

"Didn't I? Haven't I done enough for you? I paid for your schooling, got you a car, and gave you a down payment for a house. The rest was on you, darling. I can't believe you've disrupted the spiritual realm for something as trivial as this."

"Trivial! You were supposed to leave me everything! Not that tramp you married! Where is your safe deposit key? I know you left me something there."

"Oh, Missy Sue. This is just…don't you see there's more to life than money? I gave you everything I had planned to give you – while I was alive. There's nothing left for you. I gave it all to Tamara."

"What?" Missy Sue drew in her breath in one shocked gasp.

"Of course I did. That woman was the best thing that ever happened to me. She has a heart of gold and is going to open an animal sanctuary. You know she never even let me buy her a real diamond? They are manufactured stones in her ring!" Nathan laughed. "She just didn't care about that stuff. Said she'd rather use the money to donate to the puppies. Breath of fresh air, she was. Tell her I miss her and will love her always, will you? Oh, and that I'm okay if she moves on. She's young and…energetic."

I squinched my nose up at that.

"You can't be serious…" Missy Sue whispered.

"Of course I am, Missy Sue. I gave you the tools you needed to succeed. That was my job as a parent. The rest of your life has been your choices. Haven't you tried talking to your husband about this? He might help you."

"I…I…" Missy Sue was letting out little breaths of air like a steam engine. I feared the wail was coming next.

"It's time for you to grow up. Now, I'm not saying you've been a bad kid, and I've always loved you in my own way. But I knew who you were, you see? You were a user. And you always saw my money more than you ever saw me. It's too bad. Our relationship could have been a lot different."

"But…but…I loved you. You're my daddy. You were going to save me from everything!"

"Don't you see, Missy Sue? Only you can save your-self. I never had the answers for you. You'd burn through my money and move on to the next person to take advan-tage of. Never once did you try to put the work in to make something of yourself. And now? I fear it's too late for you. Best of luck. Oh, and don't forget to tell Tamara what I said."

"I will not tell that woman what you said!" Missy Sue began to shriek, and Nathan turned to me with a pained look on his face.

"I'll tell Tamara for you. I've met her before, she's really lovely."

"Thank you. Um…can you get me out of this?" Nathan looked down at the body he inhabited as Missy Sue's fit went nuclear.

"I can, sugar, no problem." Miss Elva sailed up and booped him on the head like a cheerful witch, and the body dropped to the ground. Nathan hovered over it for a moment, looking momentarily bewildered, and then nodded once to us before winking out of sight.

"I don't think she liked what she heard," I commented as Missy Sue raged to the sky.

"No, she really didn't. Here, allow me," Miss Elva said, and slapped Missy Sue clear across her face. It was enough to shock the woman into stopping the noise she was making, though she struggled to breathe as tears streamed from her eyes.

"That feels good, doesn't it?" I asked as we turned away.

"Better than I thought it would," Miss Elva agreed.

We both looked up as Trace and Chief Thomas ran through the back door and then just skidded to a stop as they took in the sheer chaos of my backyard. I couldn't even bring myself to turn around and look, the vision of the swimming zombies forever embedded in my brain, and instead I ran to Trace.

Chapter Twenty-Six

"JESUS, how many of them are there?" Chief Thomas moved his gun from body to body.

"Althea, please tell me they didn't swim here." Trace ran to my side and wrapped his arms around me. "I can't look."

"They swam here. It was awful," I said, looking up at his eyes.

"I may not sleep for weeks." Trace pulled me to him and hugged me tightly. "I'm not sure I'll ever feel safe diving again knowing that zombies can swim."

"Don't shoot them," Luna said, raising her hand to Chief Thomas. "They don't mean us harm. It's...complicated to explain. But they aren't trying to hurt us."

"I'm really going to need an explanation at some point," Chief Thomas said, his face pained. "But for now can you get rid of them?"

"Why don't you take Missy Sue in and we'll...work on cleanup. Maybe send Joseph by. With...a truck," I said, looking out at the bodies lumbering across my garden.

"Wait, no. Not my flowers, too!" I groaned as a body stumbled and landed on my plants.

"Oops," Trace said.

"I'd finally grown some things. I'm domesticating."

"We'll get you another plant."

"Althea, could you get me up to speed? And quickly?" Chief Thomas nodded to the sobbing Missy Sue.

"Missy Sue is your grave robber. She's been trying to bring dear ol' Daddy back to life," I said. "And if that's not enough to put her away for a while, I suggest looking into the disappearance of an Everglades swamp guide. She may be responsible for his death."

"Missy Sue, is this true? Have you been the one stealing bodies?"

"I just wanted to bring my daddy back," Missy Sue howled, and Chief Thomas shook his head sadly. Moving to her side, he glanced down at the cuffs and then at me.

"I've been looking for these."

"No idea." I shrugged, and he sighed. I wondered at what point he'd tire of me. But for now he seemed grateful for me to be the clean-up crew on this mess as he hauled the mess that was Missy Sue.

"Shall I... " Trace looked around helplessly.

"I think it would be awesome if you could go get Hank out of the downstairs bathroom and then maybe just take him upstairs? Spend some time with him, please? He was pretty scared when Missy Sue had a gun on me."

"A gun?" Trace took a few deep breaths.

"Hey! You got my message."

"I did. Just as I was motoring back from a dive. It was

probably the fastest I've ever driven my boat. My guests were not exactly happy with me."

"I'm sorry. But I'm glad you're here. You were smart to make me do that."

"I couldn't find your location until I was closer to shore and got better reception. I wasn't exactly helpful to Chief Thomas until I was in range."

"You did good. Now you get puppy cuddles as your reward."

"I'd say that I'm happy to stay and help here...but... " Trace looked back toward the water, where a body crawled across the shore. "Just, yeah, gross."

"It's fine. We have this handled. Thank you for coming as soon as you could."

"I'm glad you're okay," Trace said, and ran a finger down my cheek.

"Yeah, me too." I watched him walk away, grateful for his presence in my life, and happy we were on even ground again.

"Hey, cutie." A corpse leered at me.

"Ewww. Guys, seriously, we have to reverse this spell. Like now," I said as I darted away from a corpse lumbering toward me. I couldn't even bring myself to look at the water again.

"But that's the most action you've gotten in a long time," Rafe taunted me, and I whirled on him.

"You are really beginning to drive me crazy!"

"What's new? You've always been nutso." Rafe laughed and darted off. Wasn't he the daring one when Hank wasn't around to terrorize him?

"Okay, I've gotten rid of all the ones that just showed

up without trying to find a form." Miss Elva strode up from the beach, her silver caftan shining brightly in the sun.

"I don't think the rest are all that fast-moving." Luna came over from the fence and surveyed my yard. I didn't even want to think about the amount of cleanup that was needed here. I hoped Joseph would bring backup.

"What do we do?"

"We'll have to do a spell that sends them back over the line."

"Okay. And we know this spell?" I asked.

"Of course. But let's get to the circle. This is more intricate, as many spirits don't want to leave. You'll want to be very careful to stay completely focused."

"What if a zombie runs at me?"

"Just stay in the circle, Althea." Luna rolled her eyes. I saw she'd given up on trying to stop me from calling them zombies.

"I'm in it." I all but jumped in the circle she'd chalked on my back porch, ready to Be of Service. Yes, I thought that in capital letters because it was like a job description and I needed to take this seriously.

I waited as Miss Elva and Luna consulted with each other and returned to the circle with a silver bowl and a candle. I kept my back to the yard, knowing how distracted I would be if I watched the bodies destroy any more of my landscaping.

"We call to the east…" Luna began to call the elements and Miss Elva elbowed me to focus. Rafe hovered over her head, laughing at me and making mimicking motions with his hands when I got in trouble with Miss Elva. Squeezing my eyes shut, I forced myself to breathe slowly and focus on what Luna was incanting.

"For those we've called…it's in our power to send them home… "

My doorbell rang and my head popped up. Automatically, I strode to the door because I knew Joseph was here to collect the bodies.

"Althea! No!" Luna shouted, and I whirled around in time to see Rafe snap from sight.

"I just – oh shit!" I shouted. Bodies hit the ground left and right as Miss Elva regarded me with horror.

"I'm so sorry." I rushed back into the circle and looked wildly around. "Please tell me what I think happened didn't just happen."

"Oh, Althea," Luna whispered, her tone sending fear through my veins.

"Did it?" I gasped, panic racing through me, my eyes on Miss Elva's frozen face.

Rosita laughed from where she watched us from a safe distance. "It looks like you've finally sent that idiot pirate ghost back where he belongs."

"Oh no! I swear I didn't mean to. Miss Elva – you have to believe me!"

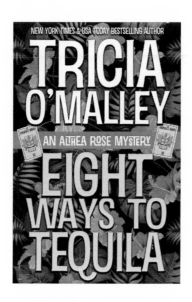

Available from Amazon

The following is a sneak peak from
Eight Ways to Tequila
Book 8 in the Althea Rose Mystery Series

Chapter One

IT WASN'T LIKE I'd meant to send Rafe across the line and through the veil that separated our world from the spirit world. It's just that, well, these things happen with me. On my best days, I'll only spill coffee on my dress. On my bad days, well, I'll screw up a magick spell or two.

Some with worse consequences than others.

Now, I wasn't going to point out that it was my tendency to make mistakes in magick that had first gifted Miss Elva with the annoyance we had come to know and love – well, tolerate – as Rafe. But now, looking at the stubborn set of her jaw, I was convinced that perhaps I should hold that little reminder in my back pocket while she worked herself down from rage.

A silent Miss Elva was a terrifying thing, that's for sure.

"We'll get him back," Luna said, stepping between the two of us like a referee ready for a cage match. "We can get him back. He can't have gone all that far."

"We can't do another spirit summoning spell this close

to the last one. It's far too dangerous," Miss Elva said. Her hands landed on her waist and I felt my shoulders hunch as I waited for her to berate me.

"We'll figure it out. We always do," Luna promised.

"Or, you know, maybe we live without him for a bit and see if we like it?"

Oops. Perhaps that wasn't the best thing to say. Miss Elva's eyes widened and she sucked in her breath, sounding like a bull about to charge. Luna turned on me, her mouth rounded in shock.

I'm Althea Rose and today might just be my last day on Earth.

Available from Amazon

Afterword

Thank you for spending time with my book, I hope you enjoyed the story.

Have you read books from my other series? Join our little community by signing up for my newsletter for updates on island-living, giveaways, and how to follow me on social media!
http://eepurl.com/1LAiz.

or at my website
www.triciaomalley.com

I hope my books have added a little magick into your life. If you have a moment to add some to my day, you can help by telling your friends and leaving a review. Word-of-mouth is the most powerful way to share my stories. Thank you.

The Isle of Destiny Series

ALSO BY TRICIA O'MALLEY

Stone Song

Sword Song

Spear Song

Sphere Song

A completed series.

Available in audio, e-book & paperback!

"Love this series. I will read this multiple times. Keeps you on the edge of your seat. It has action, excitement and romance all in one series."

- Amazon Review

The Wildsong Series

Song of the Fae

Melody of Flame

Chorus of Ashes

"The magic of Fae is so believable. I read these books in one sitting and can't wait for the next one. These are books you will reread many times."

- Amazon Review

Available in audio, e-book & paperback!

Available Now

The Siren Island Series

ALSO BY TRICIA O'MALLEY

Good Girl

Up to No Good

A Good Chance

Good Moon Rising

Too Good to Be True

A Good Soul

In Good Time

A completed series.

Available in audio, e-book & paperback!

"Love her books and was excited for a totally new and different one! Once again, she did NOT disappoint! Magical in multiple ways and on multiple levels. Her writing style, while similar to that of Nora Roberts, kicks it up a notch!! I want to visit that island, stay in the B&B and meet the gals who run it! The characters are THAT real!!!" - Amazon Review

The Althea Rose Series

ALSO BY TRICIA O'MALLEY

One Tequila

Tequila for Two

Tequila Will Kill Ya (Novella)

Three Tequilas

Tequila Shots & Valentine Knots (Novella)

Tequila Four

A Fifth of Tequila

A Sixer of Tequila

Seven Deadly Tequilas

Eight Ways to Tequila

Tequila for Christmas (Novella)

"Not my usual genre but couldn't resist the Florida Keys setting. I was hooked from the first page. A fun read with just the right amount of crazy! Will definitely follow this series."- Amazon Review

A completed series.

Available in audio, e-book & paperback!

The Mystic Cove Series

Wild Irish Heart

Wild Irish Eyes

Wild Irish Soul

Wild Irish Rebel

Wild Irish Roots: Margaret & Sean

Wild Irish Witch

Wild Irish Grace

Wild Irish Dreamer

Wild Irish Christmas (Novella)

Wild Irish Sage

Wild Irish Renegade

Wild Irish Moon

"I have read thousands of books and a fair percentage have been romances. Until I read Wild Irish Heart, I never had a book actually make me believe in love."- Amazon Review

A completed series.

Available in audio, e-book & paperback!

Also by Tricia O'Malley

Author's Acknowledgement

A very deep and heartfelt *thank you* goes to those in my life who have continued to support me on this wonderful journey of being an author. At times, this job can be very stressful, however, I'm grateful to have the sounding board of my friends who help me through the trickier moments of self-doubt. An extra-special thanks goes to The Scotsman, who is my number one supporter and always manages to make me smile.

Please know that every book I write is a part of me, and I hope you feel the love that I put into my stories. Without my readers, my work means nothing, and I am grateful that you all are willing to share your valuable time with the worlds I create. I hope each book brings a smile to your face and for just a moment it gives you a much-needed escape.

Slainté,
Tricia O'Malley

As always, you can reach me at
info@triciaomalley.com
or feel free to visit my website at
www.triciaomalley.com.

Made in United States
North Haven, CT
27 December 2023

46727700R00140